D0955756

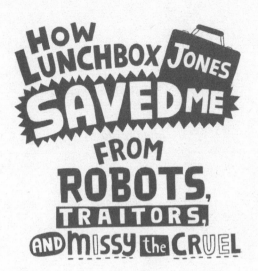

ALSO BY JENNIFER BROWN

*Life on Mars*

# HOW LUNCHBOX JONES SAVED ME FROM ROBOTS, TRAITORS, AND MISSY THE CRUEL

★ JENNIFER BROWN ★

BLOOMSBURY

NEW YORK  LONDON  OXFORD  NEW DELHI  SYDNEY

First published in the United States of America in August 2015
by Bloomsbury Children's Books
www.bloomsbury.com

Bloomsbury is a registered trademark of Bloomsbury Publishing Plc

For information about permission to reproduce selections from this book, write to
Permissions, Bloomsbury Children's Books, 1385 Broadway, New York, New York 10018
Bloomsbury books may be purchased for business or promotional use. For information on bulk
purchases please contact Macmillan Corporate and Premium Sales Department at
specialmarkets@macmillan.com

Library of Congress Cataloging-in-Publication Data
Brown, Jennifer.
How Lunchbox Jones saved me from robots, traitors, and Missy the Cruel / by Jennifer Brown.
pages     cm
Summary: Luke Abbott's school is the losing-est school in the history of losing. And that's just fine for
him. He'd rather be at home playing video games and avoiding his older brother Rob and the Greatest
Betrayal of All Time. But now he's being forced to join the robotics team,
where surely he'll help uphold the school's losing streak.
ISBN 978-1-61963-454-1 (hardcover) • ISBN 978-1-61963-455-8 (e-book)
[1. Middle schools—Fiction. 2. Schools—Fiction. 3. Brothers—Fiction. 4. Robotics—Fiction.] I. Title.
PZ7.B814224Ho 2015          [Fic]—dc23          2014019118

Book design by Nicole Gastonguay
Typeset by Westchester Book Composition
Printed and bound in the U.S.A. by Thomson-Shore Inc., Dexter, Michigan
2  4  6  8  10  9  7  5  3  1

All papers used by Bloomsbury Publishing, Inc., are natural, recyclable products
made from wood grown in well-managed forests. The manufacturing processes
conform to the environmental regulations of the country of origin.

For Scott-Bot
and
for Team #7223
*We are the 'Shakers!*
*The mighty, mighty 'Shakers!*

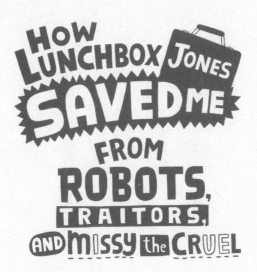

# CHAPTER 1

PROGRAM NAME: Clueless
STEP ONE: Robot grabs paper with pincers
STEP TWO: Robot eats paper
STEP THREE: Robo-burp

Rumor had it that inside the Forest Shade Middle School's mascot costume was a seventy-two-year-old woman. Coach Verde's seventy-two-year-old mom, Doris, to be exact. Made sense. While other schools' mascots tumbled and danced to rocking music, our raccoon was frequently found sitting in a rocking lawn chair knitting toilet-paper-roll covers.

Not that a real mascot would have made much difference, anyway. We Rallying Raccoons hadn't won a game in pretty much as long as anyone could remember. In any sport. Not a single one. Soccer, baseball, cheerleading, basketball, girls' gymnastics, not even a game of air hockey at the skating rink on a Friday night.

Our football team was so bad, Mrs. Balinski's classroom guinea pig, Chuck, was on the roster as tight end for two whole seasons before anyone noticed. The trophy case outside the office held only one trophy: a coffee mug with the words WORLD'S BEST SECRETARY printed on it. And the word "best" had been crossed out with marker and replaced with the words "pretty good."

In short, we were the losing-est middle school ever in the history of middle schools. It was sort of our thing.

But that never stopped the raccoon from showing up in the oddest places, trying to whip up school spirit. Waving pom-poms in the parking lot, tossing candy into the bleachers during assemblies, trying to get a conga line going in the science hallway. People mostly ignored the raccoon. Some students made fun of it. Once someone stuck a Post-it on the raccoon's back—RABID RODENT! RUN FOR IT!—causing a body jam in the cafeteria doorway.

I felt a little sorry for Old Mrs. Verde, and I tried to be nice to the raccoon. Sure, it would have been cool to have a trophy with my name on it in the trophy case—LUKE ABBOTT, FIRST-PLACE WINNER OF ALL THINGS SEVENTH GRADE—but I didn't really care about school spirit and winning and stuff. I had my own problems to deal with, mostly surrounding my brother, Rob, and the Greatest Betrayal of All Time. But why take that out on the mascot? I always grabbed the fliers the raccoon was handing out without even looking at them, just so someone would take one and make Old Mrs. Verde feel like she wasn't wasting perfectly good knitting time.

Which was why, when I came home from school one day and Dad pulled a crumpled piece of orange paper out of the middle of the wreck that is my binder, I had no clue what it was.

"What is this?" he asked, smoothing it out.

I shrugged, heading for the fridge. "I don't know."

He studied it, his brow crinkling, and then read out loud, "The Rallying Robo-Raccoons want you. Join us for an informational meeting on Monday after school, three p.m. sharp. Be there, or be an ill-fitting cog."

"That doesn't rhyme at all," I said, reaching for the orange juice. "Shouldn't it say 'be there, or be square'?"

Dad looked up from the paper. "Robotics, huh? Sounds like fun. Maybe you should go to that meeting."

"Why?"

"Why not?"

"I don't have time. I like my schedule as it is right now."

"Your schedule is coming home from school and playing video games until dinner."

"Exactly. Plus, I don't want to be the only one there with the raccoon. I don't know how to knit, and I heard if you show up she makes you try on heart sweaters and owl hats and stuff." I opened the orange juice and took a big swig directly from the bottle.

Dad dropped the paper on the counter and turned to get me a glass. "Really, it can't be as bad as all that. You never know—you might be good at robotics."

I stared at him. "Dad, have you forgotten? We are Forest

Shade Middle School. We aren't good at anything. It's our thing." Not true. I was good at some things. Like math and science. And I was really, really good at video games, especially *Alien Onslaught*. If Forest Shade had a digital-alien-destroying team, we would win every competition.

Dad took the orange juice and poured me a glass, then held one finger in the air. "You have a pretty good secretary. Says so right in the trophy case."

"That's beside the point," I said. But before I could finish, the garage door opened and in walked my older brother, Rob.

"Hey," he said to my dad as he dropped his car keys on the kitchen table. His eyes landed on me. "Hey, li'l bro. How's it going?"

I picked up my glass of orange juice and stomped out of the room as if I hadn't heard him say a word. I heard my dad say, "Still nothing, huh?" after I'd left, and Rob reply, "Nope, it's like I'm a ghost to him."

I turned on the TV and flopped on the couch. Yep, it was exactly like he was a ghost. My big brother, Rob. My "best buddy," Rob. My Got Your Back Rob. My Don't Bother to Ask Your Little Brother's Opinion Before Doing Something Life Changing and Stupid Rob. I hadn't talked to him in a whole month. Hadn't even been in the same room with him if I could help it. He was exactly like a ghost.

The kind of ghost that made me get a lump right in the center of my chest so big I could hardly even swallow my orange juice.

I scooted to the floor, picking up a controller and clamping a headset on my head. I curled up into the beanbag chair I liked to call my Ultimate Gaming Zone and switched on *Alien Onslaught.* Right away, Randy's voice filled my ear.

"Yo, Luke, what's up? Ready to defeat some aliens?"

"Yep, I left a big green one under the stairs last night after you logged off."

Randy's laughter crackled in the headset. It was loud and made me shut one eye against it, but it was drowning out Dad and Rob the Traitor, so I didn't mind too much. "What's so funny?"

I had to wait for Randy to catch his breath. "A big green one . . . Sounds like . . . you're talking about . . . a booger." He paused for more laughter, then took a breath and added, "Did you leave a big brown one in the bathroom, too?"

He cracked up again—big, yelpy laughs—and I couldn't help it. I joined him. *Big brown one in the bathroom.* That was pretty good.

I'd never seen Randy in person. We met in an epic alien battle online, and while sometimes he had this weird sense of humor, he seemed pretty cool to hang out with, even if it was only a one-eared relationship. Ever since the Rob thing happened, I needed a friend to hang with. And Randy and I had a lot in common. We both loved video games. And we both hated aliens. And . . . well, we really hadn't talked about much else. What else was there, anyway? Life got too complicated when you added other stuff into it.

We signed in and chose our characters. We played, Randy coming up with booger-related names for every alien we came across ("Look! It's Dangler!" "Here comes Old Crusty, Luke! Run!" "Uh-oh, Globby needs a tissue"), until I heard Mom's car pull into the garage and Dad call for me to pick up my stuff so he could make dinner.

I turned off the game and poked my head into the kitchen. "Is you-know-who gone?"

Dad looked up from the mushrooms he was cleaning in the sink. "Who? Oh, you mean your brother, who you were really rude to? Yes, he's gone."

"Good."

I scooped my binder and jacket into my arms and started toward my room.

"You're going to have to forgive him sometime, Luke," Dad said.

I stopped. "No, I won't."

"Yes, you will. He's your brother. And he'll be going off to boot camp in May."

I sighed. How could Dad not see that Rob going off to boot camp in May was the *problem*? How could Mom not see it? How could they just be proud of him and happy for him and not even think about what this really meant? Rob was abandoning us. For what? To be a marine? What about being a good brother who said he would always be around? What about that broken promise? Didn't that mean anything to anyone but me?

But I didn't say any of those things to Dad. He wouldn't get it.

Finally Dad just nodded his head toward the crumpled

orange paper on the counter. "Don't forget that. Be there, or be a robot," he said in a monotone robot voice.

I walked over and snatched it up. "That doesn't rhyme at all," I said. Then I took my binder to my bedroom, dropping the crumpled robotics paper into the recycling bin on my way.

# CHAPTER 2

PROGRAM NAME: Walter
STEP ONE: Robot squawks and buzzes
about its robot wheels
STEP TWO: Friend robot zones out
STEP THREE: Robot flips candy into
zoned-out friend robot's mouth—
robo-chomp!

My friend Walter met me by my locker the next day. Walter was a sixth grader, and even though some kids thought it was against the Code of Coolness for seventh graders to be friends with sixth graders, I liked Walter. He and I had one of those unique friendships—the kind where he hung around at my locker every day, waiting for me so we could talk about cars.

I knew nothing about cars.

I mean, I knew that riding in one when you wanted to get places was preferable to walking through a blizzard. I knew they had four wheels and that if your car suddenly had fewer than four wheels and you were inside it on the highway, it was probably bad. And I knew that Skittles and french fries had a life span of forever in seat cracks, and . . . Um, yeah, that was pretty much everything I knew about cars.

Walter, on the other hand, knew absolutely everything there ever was to know about cars. He was obsessed with them. He was supposedly even making something called a kit car with his uncle Reuben, which he said was like a giant model, only you didn't use glue to put it together and you could actually *drive* it. Walter was always talking about fuses and carburetors and differential something-or-others and a bunch of stuff that sounded suspiciously made up. Cars were the only thing Walter ever talked about.

I didn't mind. Walter was a really nice guy. Plus, his mom sent him to school with candy every day. Car talk was a lot easier to listen to when you had a face full of chocolate.

"Hey, Walter," I said as I twisted the dial on my lock. "How's the exciting automotive world today?"

"Dude, my uncle got the chassis for our car yesterday," he said, his black curls bouncing excitedly off his forehead.

"Awesome," I said, because I knew that saying what I really was thinking—*what the heck is a chassis?*—would lead to a car tutorial that would make me late to gym class. Unless a chassis was wrapped in Walter's mom's homemade caramel, I would wait to ask, so that it could make me late to something boring, like health class. I tossed my backpack into my locker.

"Yeah, now we're just waiting on the clutch assembly and then we can start really putting her together."

I was guessing a clutch assembly wasn't an *actual* assembly, like the kind where the raccoon mascot tries to get everyone to do the wave. "That's really cool. I can't wait to see it . . . uh, the clutch thing." Assuming a clutch thing was something one would actually see, of course.

"When the car's done, I'll ask my uncle if we can take you for a drive," Walter said. "We'll go get burgers."

Finally, he was saying something I could understand. "Sounds great. I love burgers." Bonus: I knew for sure exactly what a burger was.

We started off toward the gym. Walter didn't have first period gym, but his classroom was on the way, so we always walked together until he had to split off for the computer lab.

"Oh, hey, jelly beans?" he asked, digging in the front pocket of his backpack. "My mom sent them. They're gourmet flavors."

"Is one of them chassis flavored?"

"Huh?"

"Never mind," I said. "Just a joke." Kind of. It was also a way to make sure that a chassis wasn't some kind of food, because I still wasn't entirely sure, and it sounded kind of foody. Like a cherry chassis with chocolate sauce and nuts. That sounded delicious, actually. "Thanks." I took a handful of beans and tipped them into my mouth all at once.

"Ew," Walter said, nibbling a red bean in half.

"What?"

"All the flavors mixed up like that."

I shrugged. "It's not bad. It's kind of like fruit salad."

Walter grinned and nodded, flecks of red jelly bean

wedged in his braces. "Yeah. My mom's always bugging me to eat more fruits and vegetables," he said. He grabbed a handful of beans and tossed them all into his mouth as well. He made an *mmm* sound, but I could see him hiding a grimace beneath it. I think that was what I liked best about Walter. He was up for just about anything.

Coach Verde made us stay in our squad lines after calisthenics.

"Today, gentlemen," he said, pacing in front of us, "we will be starting our football tournament." Everyone groaned. Nothing put fear in the heart of a Forest Shade Middle School student like the word "tournament." Except for maybe "contest," "competition," "trophy," "award" . . . Okay, maybe there were a lot of words that would strike fear in the heart of a Forest Shade Middle School student.

Coach waved a paper in the air, and the moans died down. "Now, I don't want to hear any attitudes about it. This is an important unit. Intramural football starts in two weeks, and we need players for our squad."

"Did the guinea pig quit?" someone asked, and everyone snickered.

Coach gave an exasperated look. "There will be no animal entries on the team this year," he said. "All players will be human." And everyone cracked up again, because, seriously, only at Forest Shade would you hear something like that.

"I want you all to try hard out there, men," he said,

pacing in front of our lines with his hands behind his back like a drill sergeant. We rolled our eyes. Everyone knew that Coach Verde only called us "men" when he was about to put the hurt on us. Running laps, we were "guys." Running laps with high knees and the air conditioner broken, we were "men." His calling us "men" meant there would be no getting out of this tournament terror. "We need a strong football squad. Rumor has it Goat Grove may have lost its star quarterback to a wrist injury this year. And you know what that means."

A spattering of surprised murmurs echoed through the gym. Goat Grove Middle School was our official rival. The second losing-est middle school in all of Kansas City, Goat Grove's one and only win every year was against Forest Shade teams. What Coach meant was clear—with Goat Grove's star quarterback gone, maybe there would be a chance that we could finally beat them at something. Personally, I was doubtful.

He divided our squads into teams and matched us up, and we all trooped outside to play. Right away, Brian Blye got a bloody nose and had to go to the nurse. And that was before anyone even threw a ball. On the first play of the first game, three guys knocked heads all going for the same four-leaf clover and had to lie down in the grass for a few minutes. Turned out, the clover only had three leaves, anyway.

By the end of class, we were all sweaty and tired, our knees bleeding and our elbows grass stained. Jimmy Nathan had managed to sprain every finger on his left hand, Miller Standford's glasses hung askew on his face, someone broke a mobile-unit window, and Bobby Mintell's shoe went missing.

And all teams were tied 0–0.

Goat Grove had nothing to worry about.

# CHAPTER 3

PROGRAM NAME: The Mope
STEP ONE: Robot falls into pit
STEP TWO: Robot sees monster in pit
STEP THREE: Robot gets scared and drops
   cog in its robo-shorts

Life Skills class was right after lunch. Which stunk because our teacher, Mr. Terry, was a really mopey-sounding guy with a voice that pulled down on the ends of his words and made every sentence he said sound like it was falling into a pit. Even if it was a really happy sentence.

Not to mention I had yet to figure out what we were supposed to be doing in that class. Dad had told me he thought we'd probably be learning how to make budgets and balance checkbooks and figure percentages on credit cards and stuff. But so far all we'd done was watch movies and toss pencils at the ceiling tiles.

There were exactly forty-seven pencils hanging by their points in the ceiling tile above Evan Miller's desk, and Mr. Terry had no clue. It was our favorite game. We called it Pencil Stick, and the goal was to think up our best pencil-launch move and wait for Mr. Terry to turn his back so we could try it out. I proudly boasted thirteen of those forty-seven pencils myself. It was a small victory, but when you had to keep your cheering to silent pantomime, it felt huge.

But today Mr. Terry came in carrying a bucket full of jangling things. He reached the front of the room just as the tardy bell rang and dropped the box with a clang on a front-row desk. Jessie Conley, the girl sitting in that desk, jumped, spitting her gum on the floor. She let out a little squeak.

"Who here got this paper?" Mr. Terry asked. He held up the orange sheet of paper that I recognized as the one I'd recycled the night before. "Ricky Raccoon handed them out at the end of the day yesterday. Anyone?"

A boy up front raised his hand. "Who is Ricky Raccoon?"

"Our mascot, dummy," Amber Watts said, rolling her eyes.

"I thought our mascot's name was Robert," Jessie offered.

"I heard it was Rudy," Gannon Match said.

"My mom said it was Ralph," Melody Stemp added.

Steve Samuel shook his head. "Our mascot's name is Doris Verde."

Incredulous echoes of *Doris?* rang around the room.

"Doris doesn't even start with an *R*," Amber pointed out. "That makes no sense at all. Ralph sounds way better than

Doris. But it's not Ralph, either. It's Ricky. Mr. Terry should know."

"I don't see why it should have to start with an *R*," Jessie said, turning all the way around in her chair so she was facing the whole class. "There's no reason why Bruce wouldn't be a perfectly fine name for a raccoon. Or Ellen."

"Yeah," said Steve. "Or Doris. Because her name really is Doris."

"Ladies, fellas, let's get back to the subject at hand," Mr. Terry kept saying, but nobody was really listening anymore. The Great Raccoon Name Debate of Room 109 had gotten too far under way. He raised the paper into the air. "Did anyone get a flier?"

And then suddenly there was a voice.

"I got one," it said.

Only it was a really deep, strange voice that had a bit of a booming, window-rattling quality to it. So it sounded more like:

## I GOT ONE!!!

(with dead trees and birds and stuff that fell out of the sky surrounding it).

Immediately, the whole room went quiet. And it was one of those uneasy quiets, like we were all holding our breath and counting the seconds between thunder and lightning to see how close a storm was. Even Mr. Terry looked surprised. Together, as if our heads were all attached, foosball-style, we turned and gawked at the source.

"I got one," the voice repeated, and it was clearly coming from the mouth of the kid sitting at the desk in the very back of the room.

Lunchbox Jones.

Nobody had ever heard Lunchbox Jones speak. Most people thought Lunchbox Jones *couldn't* speak. That he'd lost the ability to form words when he was in the state penitentiary, perhaps. That his vocal cords had been ripped out by the mountain lion he supposedly fought with his bare hands. That he'd permanently damaged his throat while eating his old art teacher. That he'd taken a vow of silence to cover up all the murders he'd committed.

Everybody knew Lunchbox Jones, but nobody *knew* Lunchbox Jones. Not really. All we knew about him was that he carried a blue lunchbox everywhere he went and that he was pretty much always in trouble for something nobody ever saw. And that he was scary. Really, *really* scary.

### All-Time World History Ranking
### of Scariest Things That Ever Scared Anyone:

8. Snakes with fangs. Also, snakes without fangs.
7. Spiders, especially the kind that hop toward you when you get close to them with your shoe, like you messed with the beast and now it is *on* and they are about to devour you, *so bring it, bro.*

6. Clowns hiding in closets.
5. Seeing anyone you know while shopping in the underwear department of any store. Especially if the person you know is Mrs. Poole, your old music teacher from elementary school, and she stops to have a big, long conversation with your mom about how much she misses you, *while holding underwear in her hand the entire time.*
4. Sock puppets, especially the kind where one button eye is half falling off and bounces around on its sock cheek every time it moves its mouth, making your own eye suddenly feel a little bulgy and loose.
3. Movies featuring heavily breathing dudes in masks carrying unconventional weapons through foggy, wooded areas.
2. Actual serial killers.
1. Lunchbox Jones.

Lunchbox Jones had frizzy hair that went to his shoulders, and he always wore a camouflage jacket. One theory was that he wore the jacket to make it easier to stalk his prey on the walk home from school. But nobody could say for sure if his prey was of the animal or people variety. Either way, if you were sucker enough to walk your dog on Lunchbox Jones's route home from school, one of you was pretty much a goner as far as the rest of us were concerned.

Nobody had a clue what was in his blue lunchbox, but so

far Forest Shade Middle School hadn't found a student brave enough to ask. There were rumors about what might be in there—a human heart, various poisons and implements of torture, a very tiny rabid wolverine—but the only thing we could all agree on was that none of us wanted to find out for sure.

Even Mr. Terry seemed kind of stunned that Lunchbox had spoken up. He paused and stared for a moment, then swallowed and stammered, "G-goo-good. I'm g-gl-glad." Then he seemed to collect himself. He cleared his throat a bunch of times and then focused his attention on the rest of us, as, one by one, heads turned back to the front of the room. But I guess I must have been last to look away, because suddenly Lunchbox zeroed in on me, making all my guts liquify immediately. He glared and then, without warning, bared his teeth at me and snapped them together. *Clack!* Only it sounded like:

(with femurs and skulls and stuff flying out between his molars).

I gasped and quickly faced front again.

"Anyone else get a flier? Besides, er, . . . besides Mr. . . . um . . ." Mr. Terry trailed off. Even he didn't seem to know what else to call Lunchbox. Even Lunchbox's parents probably called him Lunchbox. If he had parents. Some kids believed that he was hatched in a lab experiment gone awry.

I slid down a couple of inches in my seat. No way was I going to say anything now about getting that flier.

"Well, that's okay," Mr. Terry said, though he looked a little defeated. "I have plenty of leftover fliers here. But first I thought you might like to see what robotics is about."

He reached into the box and pulled out a machine. It was silver and white, with black rubber wheels that looked like they belonged on a tank, and a bunch of wires and arms and cords sticking out in every direction. "This is our robot," he said. We all leaned forward.

"What do you do with it?" Darius Smith asked.

Mr. Terry gazed at the robot doubtfully. "Well, we program it to perform certain tasks."

"Like bring you the newspaper and mow the lawn?" Several girls giggled, and Darius looked around, like it hadn't been a joke but he was proud that it turned into one.

"Not exactly," Mr. Terry said. "More like to knock little bowling pins down with a Ping-Pong ball or push a block into a square."

Jessie made a face. "That's all?"

"You make that awesome robot, and all it does is push a block into a square?" Amber said, and Mr. Terry nodded.

"Do you get to take down any bad guys in the square, at least?" Gannon asked.

Mr. Terry's mouth drifted down to super-mope. "It's very exciting."

"It doesn't sound very exciting," Darius said.

"It sounds really boring," Jessie added. "I agree with Gannon. Bad guys are way cooler than a block and a square." There were murmurs of agreement.

"Here. I'll run a program for you. You'll see," Mr. Terry said. He leaned over the robot and fiddled with some buttons, then scratched his head and fiddled with the buttons some more. Finally, he stood, took the robot to the work-table at the side of the room, hit one last button with great flourish, and stood back with his hands on his hips.

We all leaned forward, our eyes trained on the robot. It whirred to life, lifted a few centimeters on its wheels, made a sound like parts spinning, revved up, and moved forward about two inches.

Then it flopped over on its side and abruptly powered off with a *pop!* and a puff of smoke.

We were all silent for a moment, staring at the dead robot. Mr. Terry scratched his head.

"Was it supposed to do that?" Jessie finally asked.

"Definitely not," Amber said, waving her hands in front of her face. "It smells."

Steve laughed, waving his hand around, too. "You programmed your robot to fart, Mr. T.?"

The class erupted into laughs that turned into dramatic coughs as we all began waving our hands in front of our faces. We were all laughing and coughing and talking so loudly, we barely heard the bell ring.

Mr. Terry picked up the robot forlornly. "Class dismissed."

# CHAPTER 4

PROGRAM NAME: Pressure
STEP ONE: Robot bumps into wall
STEP TWO: Wall bumps back
STEP THREE: Robot bangs its head on wall
    until ear gear falls off

"Mr. Abbott, may I see you for a moment?"

I had been happily heading out to the car rider line after school, bending and flexing my fingers as warm-up for alien battles with Randy. I turned at the sound of my name. Mr. Terry was trotting after me, his too-short tie bouncing up and hitting him in the chin with every step. I stopped, inwardly groaning. Getting held up after the final bell by a teacher when you could literally see your escape vehicle right there at the curb was torture. Sort of like being let out of jail only to find that the door was jammed and you'd have to wait for the locksmith to get there. And while you're waiting, they find other stuff to put you back in jail for.

Mr. Terry was out of breath by the time he reached me, and he had to take a minute to recover. I could see Dad craning his neck toward us. He probably thought I was in trouble.

Wait. *Was* I in trouble? Had Mr. Terry finally looked up at the ceiling tile? Oh, great. I was about to get reamed right in front of my dad. Double trouble. *Just put me back in jail, please!*

I held up my hands. "I swear, only thirteen of the pencils are mine. I've been having a trajectory problem because of Amber's new super-puffy hairdo."

A look of confusion crossed Mr. Terry's face, but he shook it away. "I wanted to talk to you about robotics."

Oh. He must have seen the raccoon hand me the flier, and he knew I'd been lying in class earlier by not admitting to having gotten one. "I forgot all about the flier," I blurted. "Well, I didn't really forget. It's just that Lunchbox Jones is scary and I like my schedule the way it is." In my head, that made perfect sense.

The confusion on Mr. Terry's face deepened, and it occurred to me that maybe I just needed to stop talking altogether.

"I was thinking you'd be a great fit for the team," he said. "We start next Monday right after school. Will you consider coming?"

Now it was my turn to look confused. Or maybe not so much confused as completely shocked and mystified.

Nobody had ever wanted me on a team before. "Why?" I asked.

"Why what?"

"Why do you want me? I don't know anything about robots."

"Because I think you would be an asset to our team," he said. I raised one eyebrow, and he let out a sigh. "Okay, listen, I'll level with you. We haven't won a robotics tournament in . . ." He paused, tapped his chin thoughtfully. "Ever. We have never won. And I've heard through the grapevine that you're something of a video game master."

"What grapevine?" I said. "Who called me that?" Video game master? Me? Who would have said such a thing? Of course . . . I'd never thought about it before, but I was sort of masterful. I did have my mastering moments. I cleared my throat. "I mean, not that it's not true. I do have a pretty good system, especially when it comes to the pod creatures. You see, I take the controller and . . ."

Mr. Terry sighed. "Okay, I overheard you say something to Walter about it once, that you like to play video games. And I talked to Mrs. Henley and Ms. Borchevic, and they both said you're doing really well in your math and science classes."

"I'm not exactly a master of math and science," I said. "Well, not unless Mrs. Henley and Ms. Borchevic said . . ."

"Do you like computers, Luke?" Mr. Terry interrupted.

I shrugged. "Sure. Who doesn't?"

He beamed. "See? You're perfect. We need someone who can lead us to a win, and I think that someone might be you,

Luke Abbott." He poked a finger in my chest when he said that last part. I rubbed my sternum where he'd just poked.

"But I don't know anything about robots. Or leading. Or winning."

He sighed again, scratched his mustache, and looked around elaborately before leaning in and putting an arm around my shoulders conspiratorially. "Okay, you're right. The truth is, I need warm bodies. We haven't won a game ever, and Principal McMillan is threatening to pull the plug on the program. I bought that robot with my own money, Luke. Do you know how much a robot costs?"

"Um . . . thirty bucks?"

"That was a rhetorical question, Luke. You're not supposed to answer those. And, no, nowhere near thirty bucks. A lot more than thirty bucks. I was told Forest Shade would never win anything, but I was certain, Luke. I was certain that a robotics program would pull Forest Shade out of its losing slump. I thought it would turn everything around, and soon we'd be the school to beat. I would be a hero, Luke. The hero of Forest Shade Middle School. But we haven't turned anything around. And we're running out of chances. Principal McMillan isn't going to fund a robotics team forever, Luke. Do you know how much it costs to keep a robotics team up and running? Even a losing one?"

"Um . . ." That seemed like another one of those rhetorical things he'd talked about, so I didn't answer.

"A lot." He patted me on the back and straightened up. "So you understand?"

"Yes," I said. "Totally."

"You get why I asked you?"

"I suppose so."

"And I'll see you Monday after school for our first practice?"

"No."

He frowned.

"I get it, Mr. Terry, I totally do. But I like my schedule the way it is." I reached up and patted him on the shoulder the same way he'd just done to me. "Good luck putting together your team, Mr. Terry. See you tomorrow! Oh, and just forget what I said about the pencils. I didn't know what I was talking about."

I turned and headed for Dad's car.

"Hey, buddy," Dad said as I slid in. "What was that all about?"

"Nothing," I said. "Mr. Terry needed to ask me something."

"About what?"

"Nothing important. Just robotics."

"Why would he be asking you about robotics?"

"No reason. We can go now." I clicked on my seat belt, settled back in my seat, and closed my eyes, my fingers twitching around an imaginary video game remote. Another long day, done. *Aliens, beware, Lucky Shot Luke, newly titled video game master, is coming home to the Ultimate Gaming Zone.*

Dad started to put the car into gear, but we were both startled by a knock on the window. I opened one eye to see Mr. Terry standing there, rapping with his knuckles.

I rolled down the window slowly, letting in the sounds of school buses and doom.

Mr. Terry looked over my head. "Hello, Mr. Abbott, I was wondering if I might speak to you about something for just a moment."

"Sure," Dad said, glancing at me uncertainly. I shrugged, tried to mouth, *He's crazy. We should call the police!* But he wasn't watching anymore.

"I was just talking to Luke here about our robotics program. I think he has the potential to be a great asset to our team."

Dad glanced at me again, only this time he looked proud. Not good. "Really? Well, that's wonderful news. . ."

I slid even deeper into my seat, squinching my eyes shut and wishing that this wasn't happening. When teachers and parents got together and started saying things about your potential, your free time was pretty much a dead duck.

"And we just happen to have space for new members," Mr. Terry said. "A rare opportunity for the students."

"You don't say. What luck!"

"And I thought Luke might want to get his application in before the rush of interested students . . ."

I tuned them out, wishing with everything I had that they would stop talking. But they didn't.

Ten minutes later, I was officially a member of the Forest Shade Middle School Rallying Robo-Raccoons.

# CHAPTER 5

PROGRAM NAME: The Aws
STEP ONE: Bots enter house
STEP TWO: Bots make lots and lots of
   noise
STEP THREE: Bots go after programmer's
   cheeks with pincers and squeeze

It was a Friday night. Most of my friends rejoiced on Friday nights. For them, Friday night meant going to the movies or the mall or football games and parties. For Randy, it meant unlimited alien-destruction time. For Walter, Fridays were for tinkering around in a car wonderland with his uncle.

For me, Friday nights meant the invasion of the *aws*.

Forever ago, my mom and dad were next-door neighbors. This was before my mom started wearing glasses and my dad started complaining about people leaving lights on in rooms that nobody was in. They were friends when they were kids, and then they started dating when they were teenagers, and after college my dad literally married the girl next door.

Because of this, their parents—all my grandparents— were friends. Best friends. In fact, they still lived next door to one another. They were so close, it was nearly impossible to see one set of them without the other. They were "the grand- mas and the grandpas," or sometimes "the mamaws and the papaws," or even "the maws and the paws," or, as I'd called them since I learned to talk, simply "the aws."

The maws half of the aws was made up of two busy ladies who looked remarkably alike. They were both short with tiny hands and feet, and both had curly white hair. They both talked all the time, sometimes even saying the same thing at the same time, and they both came at you with cheek-pinching claws whenever they saw you. The only way to tell them apart was that Mom's maw, Maw Shirley, always wore an apron and kept butterscotch candies in the front pocket. Dad's maw, Maw Mazie, didn't like butterscotch and always complained to Maw Shirley that she should carry cinnamon candies, instead.

The two paws were as different as the maws were alike. Dad's paw, Paw Stanley, was like Dad, tall and skinny with red hair and a big nose. Mom's paw, Paw Morris, was short, fat, and shiny bald. Paw Stanley had been a gym teacher, so he was always making up game plans and patting his chest looking for a whistle that was no longer there. Paw Morris had been a salesman, so he basically did nothing but shake hands with people and offer deals.

For my entire life, the aws came over on Friday nights for dinner—which the maws cooked together—and for cable TV sports channels—which the paws watched together—and for talking, which they all did together. And sometimes over one another. And sometimes without even breathing. It was like watching a science fiction movie: *Attack of the Nonbreathing Chatterers*.

"There's my wittle baby-waby Lukey-Wukey," Maw Shirley said the minute she walked through the door. Her hands were already outstretched in pinch formation. "Come let Mamaw get a hold of you."

Just thinking about it made my cheeks tingle. Especially since right behind her was Maw Mazie, her hands in identical pinch formation. Definitely a science fiction movie: *Attack of the Pinching Lobstermaws*.

"Just look at that sweet baby boy," Maw Mazie said, coming at me. *Pinch, pinch, pinch.*

It was useless to try to get away. The maws would get you no matter what it took. I accepted my fate, squeezed my eyes shut, and trudged toward them, sweet baby-boy cheeks–first. Even though I strongly disagreed that I was a sweet baby anything.

"Well, look at him, Maw, he gets bigger every Friday."

"I think you're right, Maw, he's a little weed, my Lukey-Wukey."

Ugh. Lukey-Wukey. I didn't mind nicknames, but Lukey-Wukey didn't exactly inspire tough alien-dispatching badness. If Randy heard me being called Lukey-Wukey, my life would pretty much be over. And his laugh would blow my eardrums right out of my head.

They hugged, they pinched, they fussed and cooed, and then Mom came into the room.

"You're here! We should get started. I was thinking Italian tonight," she said, and the maws peeled away. Mom distracted the maws for me every Friday so I wouldn't suffer permanent cheek damage. This is, in my opinion, just one of the reasons moms are awesome.

Immediately the maws began talking over each other.

"Oh, I'll handle the sauce. I'm great with sauce."

"I'll take care of the meatballs."

"We're having meatballs?"

"Well, of course we're having meatballs. It's Italian. What's more Italian than meatballs?"

As they bustled into the kitchen, Mom patted me on the shoulder. "Go on out into the living room and say hi to the paws."

The paws talked just as much as the maws. And just as loud. And just as constantly. But at least they talked about quarterbacks and baseball games and soccer plays and things that had nothing to do with hair appointments, dead people, or how my bottom used to fit into the palm of one of their hands when I was a baby. And they never touched my cheeks.

I walked into the living room. Dad was already camped in his recliner, feet up, one toe peeking out of a hole in his sock. The paws were taking up the entire couch, in matching postures—feet crossed out in front of them, one arm slung over the back of the couch, the other hand absently scratching their bellies.

They were busy arguing over the NFL draft and didn't even notice that I'd drifted into the room. I liked it that way. I pulled out the Ultimate Gaming Zone and sank down into it. I hoped they wouldn't notice me, because when they did, one of them always asked when I was going to start playing sports.

"Oh, hey there, Lukester! When we gonna see you on the gridiron, huh?"

Shoot. They noticed me.

"Yeah, you're a fireplug of a boy," Paw Morris chimed in. He hunched his chest over all muscle-like and made a grimacing face that was fairly terrifying. A guy should never have to see that many of his grandpa's teeth at once.

"We played football in gym this week," I said, hoping that would be enough to satisfy them.

"There ya go," Paw Stanley crowed, throwing his hands up. "Bet you were the star. Quarterback? Wide receiver?"

"Nah," Paw Morris said, still hunched over. "Boy that size has defensive lineman written all over him. Right, Luke? Tell your paw, you were smashmouthing, you were laying those fellas out!"

"I don't think so ... I didn't understand anything that you just said."

The paws burst into laughter, punching each other on their shoulders. "You hear that? You hear what he said? Such a jokester, our Lukeman. Didn't understand a word ... Ho-ho-ho, that boy is a real cut-up."

"Ah, good one, Luke. So tell us, what position were you?" Paw Stanley said. His fingers fidgeted over his imaginary coach's whistle excitedly.

I licked my lips. "Um, I was over by the foreign language trailers? Kind of . . . kind of by the parking lot."

The paws looked at each other confusedly, then burst into laughter again. "I tell you, Charlie," one of them said to my dad, "you've got yourself a real comedian here. By the parking lot, he says."

Dad grinned like he got the joke, so I grinned, too, and even squeezed out a little laugh.

When they'd laughed themselves out and had gone back to their appointed football-watching positions, Dad spoke up. "Did I tell you, Paw? Luke here is on a different sort of team."

"Oh, yeah?" Paw Stanley said. "Rugby?"

"I've always loved rugby," Paw Morris said. "Used to be I could get you a great deal on some rugby uniforms."

"No, not quite rugby," Dad said. "It's a robotics team."

Instantly, I felt my ears burn. This always happened when I was surprised or embarrassed—every blood cell in my whole body rushed directly to my ears, making them bright red and hot. *Please, please*, I thought, *don't let one of the maws come in and see my ears.* We would be stuck in a half-hour debate about fevers and rash-inducing illnesses from the early 1900s, and then next thing I knew I'd be rushed off to sit in some emergency room cubicle. Diagnosis: humiliated to death. Don't think it hasn't happened before.

But the maws were still in the kitchen, busily squabbling about marinara. I was safe.

The paws, however, had both gone slack jawed and were staring at me.

"Ro-what-ics?" Paw Morris asked.

"Robotics," Dad said proudly, and if I could have had any wish in the world come true, it would have been for my dad to suddenly lose his voice. Not forever; just until the paws went home. Or, even better, if I could've turned back time to the football conversation. I'd have made up a better position, like thrower or point getter or maybe something passably violent sounding like nose ruiner or arm breaker or chief mangler.

"What's that?" Paw Stanley asked.

"Sounds like some futuristic mumbo jumbo to me," Paw Morris said.

"Robots? That's not a sport," Paw Stanley said.

"Well, no," Dad said. "It's, you know, science and technology and stuff. Tell them, Luke."

I shook my head. "I don't want to do robotics," I said.

The paws looked equal parts confused and angry. "Well, you heard him, Charlie. He doesn't want to do it. Why would you pull the boy out of football to make him do something he doesn't want to do?"

"Who would want to mess around with nuts and bolts when there's a perfectly good pigskin to toss?" Paw Stanley asked.

"That's what I'm thinking. Can't blame the boy for missing his team on the field," Paw Morris declared.

"He was never in football," Dad said, and I sank deeper into the Ultimate Gaming Zone. This was just getting worse.

Paw Stanley looked very confused. "What do you mean, he was never in it?"

"Well, now you're just talking nonsense. Hey," Paw Morris said, elbowing Paw Stanley. "He's ribbing us again. You two are jokers tonight, Charlie. A fireplug like this kid not playing football but messing around with some robot nonsense instead. Ho-ho-ho! That's a good one."

Paw Stanley joined in the laughter. Dad and I stared at each other for a minute, and then Dad shrugged and started laughing along with the paws. He must have figured they had about as good a chance of understanding futuristic robot mumbo jumbo as I did of understanding one of Walter's car parts.

They all laughed and elbowed and sputtered, practically rolling around on the floor, and I felt that maybe I should start laughing, too, but right as I tried to muster up a chuckle, Rob walked into the room.

"Hey, paws, what's so funny?" he asked.

"Heeey!" the paws cried out in unison, both of them flinging their arms out hug-style.

"There's our soldier!"

"Here comes a good marine!"

"Ten-hut!"

"At ease, soldier! At ease!"

I rolled my eyes. Everyone was always making such a huge deal about Rob going into the marines. It was sickening.

It was boring. It was . . . going to happen whether I liked it or not, and that was what I liked least about it.

"I've got to go," I said, but everyone was so busy talking to Rob they didn't even hear me. I jumped up out of the Ultimate Gaming Zone and raced to my bedroom. I even gave my door a good slam, and still nobody noticed. Of course not. Just because Rob was a soldier, all of a sudden he was a star.

Rob had always been with me through everything. Through the time I wrecked my bike and had to get stitches in my forehead. Through the time when Susan Stoffsetter kissed me and I needed a deep cootie cleansing. Through the time when Walter invited me to a car show and I needed an excuse to get out of it. Everything.

But now I was stuck on a robotics team and would be forced to be with Mr. Terry and who knew who else after school every Monday with no way out. And Rob wouldn't be there.

Some star.

# CHAPTER 6

PROGRAM NAME: Group Torture
STEP ONE: Robot enters room
STEP TWO: Robot stands around looking
   goofy
STEP THREE: Robot wishes five o'clock
   would get here already

Everybody was all about hating Mondays. The kids at school complained about Mondays, rubbing their tired eyes. The teachers sighed that Mondays were so hard.

My dad spent most of Monday mornings grumbling about mountains of laundry and grocery shopping, while swigging coffee from an old Snoopy cup that read: I DON'T DO MONDAYS.

Mom rushed about with one high heel on and one off, one arm in a suit jacket and the other stuck in her briefcase handle, griping about how she had meetings all day and what could make a Monday worse than back-to-back meetings. Even Dad's signature buttery cinnamon toast couldn't make Mom stop hating Mondays.

To me, Monday seemed like pretty much any other day. Get up earlier than you want to, go to school longer than you want to, eat less lunch than you want to, go home later than you want to, and start rounding up slimy green aliens with Randy until dinner, which is the only thing you actually want to do. What was there to hate? I didn't get it.

Until the Monday of the first robotics meeting.

My brain tried to fool me. For most of the day, I was convinced that it was a Monday just like any other Monday. I'd even used most of English class to devise a plan for how Randy and I could beat level 17. (Hint: toss a pancake into the cornfield and wait for the aliens to swarm. No outer space creature could resist a good pancake. It was a proven fact.) My brain had me so good and fooled about what day it was, it took me a few minutes of waiting outside after the final bell, wondering where Dad was, before it occurred to me that I had something else to do.

"Hey, Luke, where are you going?" Walter asked as I trudged past him. He was heading out to the bus lot, a Butterfinger melting over his fingers.

"Robotics."

"Oh, that sounds like fun," he said.

"Not as fun as alien games," I grumbled.

"You want the other half?" he asked, holding out a broken piece of his Butterfinger. I was so bummed my stomach didn't even want it. I took it, anyway, and ate it in three bites, because free candy was free candy, and I didn't want to be rude to Walter. The buses roared to life outside and Walter jumped. "Well, I guess I'll see you tomorrow. Have fun with the boop-beep-bop-boop." He made a few jerky arm movements as he pushed through the doors.

Something else to hate about robotics: it suddenly made everyone you knew imitate bad robots from 1970s movies.

I kept trudging, now thirsty because of the candy but too annoyed to even bother to get a drink.

Mr. Terry was standing outside the classroom, waving me in, his glasses sliding down his nose with every movement. He pushed them back up on his face.

"Luke! Glad you could make it. That makes almost everyone. Go on in and get acquainted."

I walked through the door and dropped my backpack on the first chair.

At the front of the room, huddled around the box Mr. Terry had brought in last week, were five kids.

One of them turned when I walked in. "Oh, Luke Abbott's here," she said, and then turned back and stuffed her foot into the box of robot parts.

Mikayla Armitage, normal-looking seventh grader by day, toe prodigy by night. That was Mikayla's big claim to fame—she could do things with her toes. She was on the news once, in fourth grade, for having a whole art exhibit of paintings she made by clutching the paintbrush between her toes. She could eat, clap, and write with her feet. She wore flip-flops year round, just in case the mood to flex her feet struck, and on the first day of school you could always count on Mikayla showing off her newest toe skill. This year it had been flossing, which grossed out all the girls and got Mikayla called to the nurse's office for a discussion about things we shouldn't put in our mouths. Rumor had it she was working on basketball for next year; she just couldn't quite figure out how to dribble and run at the same time. Which was true for most of Forest Shade Middle School's basketball team, so she should fit right in.

The toe thing was kind of cool, but mostly it was weird trying to talk to someone who is brushing her hair with her feet.

I walked up to the group and stared into the box with them. If robotics was all about standing around staring at robot parts, so far it looked like we were going to do great.

"Hey," a kid next to me said. "I'm Jacob. Sixth grade."

"Oh," I said. "Hey."

Another kid sidled up to my other side. "Hey," he said. "I'm Jacob. Sixth grade."

My mouth dropped open and my head whipped back and forth between the two of them. "Uh . . ." was all I could manage.

"We're not twins," the first Jacob said.

"We're not related at all," the other one said. "My last name is Davis."

"And mine is David. Big difference."

I squinted. They both wore brown T-shirts and blue jeans. They both had blond hair and green eyes. They even both had lopsided smiles.

"It's only a one-letter difference, actually," Mikayla said. She picked up a robot piece with her toes and inspected it, then dropped it back into the box.

"Whatever," both Jacobs said at the same time.

It hurt my head.

I skirted around to the other side of the box and shoved in beside Stuart Hicks. Stuart was friends with Walter and would sometimes sit with us at lunch. But Stuart never actually bought any lunch. Instead, he ate what seemed to be an endless supply of sunflower seeds out of his jacket pocket. His mouth always bulged with seeds, and sometimes he spit the shells right onto Walter's lunch tray. Other times he would crunch the seeds up in his teeth, shells and all. I wasn't sure which was worse, but it all gave me that day-before-the-flu-hits feeling in my stomach. I secretly hated it when Stuart sat with us.

"I think I've figured out how we can win," Stuart said, his mouth working around what looked like roughly nine hundred million sunflower seeds.

"We haven't even built the robot yet," Mikayla said.

"So?" the Jacobs said in unison.

"It can't be that hard, can it?" I said. "I mean, you just put some stuff together and push a button, right?"

I heard a grunt from behind me. "Ugh. Of course, you would think that, Luke Abbott. And, gross, your ears are dirty."

I rubbed my fingers behind my ears before my brain could catch up. I knew that voice. That was the voice that had poured ice water through my veins since I was six years old. That voice was behind the recess rhyme: *Loser Luke eats his glue-k, and then goes puke. And eats that, too-k.*

I probably don't really need to point this out, but that didn't really rhyme all that well.

And it was mean.

And also? I only tried glue one time. It looked like melted marshmallows and kind of smelled tangy and I was hungry and I put a little dab on my finger and can't a guy be curious for one second of his life without some girl making a rhyme about it?

Everyone sang the Loser Luke Eats His Puke song for all five years of elementary school. They even made a jump-rope routine out of it. The all-time record of pukes I ate, according to jump-rope tallying, was forty-four, held by Holly Asanti, who swore she could have gone on had the recess whistle not been blown.

And the voice that had started that rhyme was right behind me now.

I squeezed my eyes shut and prayed I'd imagined it. Like a flashback in a horror movie.

"Gross, I'll bet you eat your ear dirt, too," the voice continued. It got closer and I felt a thump on the back of my shoulder.

*Please, no, please, no, please.* I opened one eye and chanced a look, and there she was.

Missy Farnham.

Otherwise known as Missy the Cruel.

Picture a sixth grade girl in a tenth grade boy's body. Giant, scabby knees and hands like clubs. Brown pigtails curved up like a Viking hat. Teeth that crushed the bones of small animals and freckles that spelled out the word GROWL on her cheeks.

That was pretty much the opposite of Missy the Cruel. She was tiny, with skinny legs and dimples. Her pigtails hung straight down her back in perfect little lines, and her freckles didn't spell out anything. She was, to me, a rabbit-eating ogre. She was, to the rest of the world, adorable.

I looked down, down, down at her dainty little face. "I don't eat ear dirt," I said.

She rolled her eyes. "It's not nice to lie, Luke. Lying Luke. Luke the Liar. Liaruke. I've seen you do it."

"You have not ever seen me eat my ear dirt!" I said, probably a little too loudly, because the Jacobs backed away a step.

Stuart stared at me. "Dude," he said, a sunflower seed slipping out the corner of his mouth and falling down his shirt, "that's gross."

I shuddered. Missy the Cruel, Toezilla, the sunflower boy, and the nonidentical identical Jacobs? This was going to be a very long season.

"Maybe we should just get to work," I said, diving into the box of bot parts, trying not to imagine my hands getting coated with foot-sweat particles.

"Now, that's what I like to hear," Mr. Terry said, coming into the room. He clapped his hands twice. "We've got a bot to build and program." He rubbed his hands together the way the paws sometimes do when the maws bring out big platters of food.

Mr. Terry squeezed in between the Jacobs and leaned over the box of parts with his hands on his hips. He hoisted his pants and then picked up a plastic brick. "This, my friends, is the motor. This is what will power our bot to do all the things it needs to do."

"It's just a dumb block," Missy said. She leaned over to me and whispered, "Like your head."

I glared at her.

"Yes," Mr. Terry said. "But we're going to add to it. That's what all these parts are for. We'll add arms and sensors."

"And feet?" Mikayla asked. She splayed her toes out and waved them over the box. "I think our bot should have feet. Feet are very useful."

"Er, it probably won't have feet," Mr. Terry said. "But, of course, that's entirely up to you. This is your team. I'm just here to make sure you don't burn down the school. Oh, and here's the rest of the team now!"

We all looked up just in time to see a great hulking shadow blot out the doorway and choke the sun out of existence.

"What?" the shadow said, only it boomed like:

## WHAT?!?!

(with eardrums bursting and power poles snapping in half and stuff).

"Is that . . . ?" a Jacob whispered.

"Lunchbox Jones," the other Jacob finished in a low, ominous voice.

Sure enough, the shadow emerged into the room, wearing a camouflage jacket and carrying a bright-blue lunchbox.

Correction. Missy the Cruel, Toezilla, the sunflower boy, the two nonidentical identical Jacobs . . . and Lunchbox Jones.

This wasn't just going to be a very long season; this was going to be the last season of my life.

# CHAPTER 7

PROGRAM NAME: Building Disaster
STEP ONE: Bot tries to build second bot
STEP TWO: Building bot picks up pieces
    and stares blankly at them
STEP THREE: Building bot gives up and
    jams pieces up own nose

"What's that?" Walter said as I wrestled the parts box into my locker for the hundredth time since Monday's meeting. The box was dented and beat up, a corner of the cardboard ripped. He held out a white bag and beamed. "Peanut cluster?"

I reached in and grabbed a handful of candy. I stuffed one into my mouth and smiled. I loved Peanut Cluster Friday, and Walter's mom had really outdone herself this time.

"It's a robot," I said. We headed toward our first classes.

"Didn't look like a robot," Walter said. "Looked like a bunch of plastic pieces and sunflower seeds. And it kind of smelled like feet."

"It's not technically a robot yet. I have to build one," I said.

"How?"

I stopped, reached into the bag again, and thought. "Actually, I have no idea."

I wasn't even sure how I got nominated to build it. One minute we'd all been sharing a group tremble over the terror of having to call Lunchbox Jones our teammate, and the next I'd been walking out the door, promising the group I'd have a robot ready by our next practice. It wasn't until I found myself shoving the box into the tiny space at the bottom of my locker that I realized what I'd done. I basically knew three things in this world:

1. Cheeseburgers
2. Strategies for avoiding girls' birthday parties
3. How to hack into the glitches in the *Alien Onslaught* program for maximum cheatability (which, Randy and I agreed, isn't cheating if you know how to beat the actual game)

**Note:** There used to be a 4th thing I knew—the complete and total awesomeness of my brother, Rob—but that has since been removed from the official list, for obvious reasons.

**Also note:** How to build robots was not anywhere on that list.

"You could get a book," Walter said. He pointed at the library, which we were just passing.

"A robot-building book?"

He shrugged, his long curls bouncing on his shoulders. "Why not? I have books on how to build cars. My mom has books on how to garden. My dad learned how to say *Does this celery smell rotten to you?* in five different languages out of a book. Surely there are books about building robots."

I peered through the library door. The librarian smiled and waved at me. My ears burned and I started walking again. "Maybe later," I said. "I have to get to gym. Besides, I haven't even tried anything with it yet. I bet I can figure it out without any help."

"Yeah, probably. It was a bad suggestion. Last one?" Walter said, shaking the bag.

"Nah, that one's yours."

He pulled out the last candy, shoved it into his mouth, wadded up the bag, and tossed it into a trash can. "I'll bet it's way fun to build robots," he said.

I stopped in the gym doorway and gave him what Dad calls one of my You've Got to Be Kidding looks. "The parts smell like feet," I said.

Walter shrugged. "Yeah, there's that, I guess."

"Great news, men!" Coach called as he strode across the gym to where we were sitting in our squads. "The Goat Grove quarterback is definitely out for the season! Broken wrist!" He clapped his hands enthusiastically, then seemed to catch himself and bowed his head. "I mean, it's a terrible sorrow and we all should send him well wishes that he heals quickly. But otherwise, great news!" He clapped his hands so hard his whistle bounced up and down on his chest. I couldn't help thinking of Paw Stanley and how he'd have loved to get his hands on that whistle.

Ten minutes later, we were, predictably (because he called us "men"), feeling the pain. By my count, we had four bloody knees, two turned ankles, and seven guys who'd plain given up on life. Also, someone walked into the back of a parked car on the way outside and the car alarm was busting out all our eardrums.

"Coach Verde?" Radford Perry asked, panting, lying on the ground next to the goal post. "Can I ask you a question?"

"Shoot," Coach said, still trying to sound enthusiastic, but only sounding as tired as we all felt.

"Why are we doing this?"

"I've already told you. The Goat Grove quarterback is out for the season. It's our shot. Wouldn't a trophy look good in that trophy case up front?"

"We have a trophy case? At this school?" someone asked.

"Of course we do," Coach said. "And you could be the first ones to put a trophy in it. Wouldn't that be great?"

We all gazed at one another. A few guys shook their heads. A few others coughed and held tissues over their bloody noses. The car alarm continued bleating. I was getting a headache.

"Now, who thinks they'd like to give the football team a try?" Coach asked, bouncing up and down on his toes.

"Come on, don't be shy. We'll start practice on Monday. Who's excited?"

Again with the gazing, the coughing, the car alarm. Some pitiful groaning provided a lovely melodic backbeat. If Forest Shade Middle School had an official theme song, that would have been it. I started writing lyrics in my head:

*We are Forest Shade, we live in fear.*

*We're not mighty! That is very clear.*

*If you want to beat us, all you have to do is show up* . . . wait, no, that doesn't rhyme . . . *appear! All you have to do is appear.*

*Because we are the raccoons. Anyone can kick our* . . .

"You. Luke Abbott, can I count you in?"

I jumped, looked around. I realized I was the only one still on my feet.

Rookie mistake. There were two general rules of thumb if you didn't want to be singled out in a class. Don't stand out, no matter what. Wear shirts the same color as the cinder block walls if you have to. Or if the blending-in thing isn't working for you, try method number two: volunteer for everything, no matter what, so the teacher gets tired of you and starts looking for someone else to torture.

In neither of those rules of thumb do you stand around on the football field looking like the only guy who doesn't have a broken bone.

"I can't," I said. I held one foot off the ground gingerly, like a bone had suddenly sprung a crack.

"Say, you're Rob Abbott's brother, aren't you?"

"Yes, sir."

"I hear he's going into the marines this summer."

I took a deep breath. "Yes, sir."

"Well, a good marine like that must have a brother who plays football."

I felt my eyes narrow. *Good marine. Good marine, good marine, good marine.* Didn't anyone ever talk about anything else?

"No, sir," I said, clenching my fists.

"Well, why not?" he asked.

"Because," I said. "Because I'm on the robotics team."

Well, at least robotics was good for something.

The last bell of the day had rung, and I was on my way to the front door when I saw Lunchbox Jones standing by my locker. Actually, he was standing directly in front of my locker, his arms crossed over his chest. His lunchbox dangled at his side.

My whole body went numb from the waist down. Was I walking? I didn't think I was walking. I didn't want to be walking. Because if I was walking, that would mean I was stupid enough to be moving toward Lunchbox Jones and surely I wasn't stupid enough to be doing that.

But I looked down at my feet and, sure enough, that was exactly what they were doing.

I tried to just keep going, pretend I didn't see him, pretend I didn't need to get my history notes out of my locker to study for Monday's test. I'd just take an F. No big deal.

Nowhere near as big a deal as occupying the same breathing space as Lunchbox Jones, who might decide my tongue looked like it would make a really great bow tie.

But he wouldn't let me get past.

"Hey," he said. "You."

And, of course, that was when my feet finally decided to stop moving. Really, feet? Couldn't you even be half as smart as Mikayla's feet?

"Me?" I said, trying not to twitch.

"Yeah, you. You finish that robot yet?"

"What robot? I mean, no. I mean, of course I have. It's, um, it's at my house. Cleaning. It's cleaning my room. I programmed it to do that. And stuff." It began to dawn on me that perhaps my feet weren't the only part of my body not as smart as Mikayla's feet. I willed my eyes not to drift to my locker, where, of course, the robot really was. It was like I was afraid that Lunchbox would suddenly grow x-ray vision and see it in there. And then wad me up like one of Walter's candy wrappers and toss me in the trash.

"Okay," Lunchbox said. He pushed away from my locker and began walking—slowly and scarily sauntering in that slow, scary Lunchbox way—down the hall.

Okay? *Okay?* That was it? Just okay? I almost died, and all he had to say for himself was okay?

I waited for him to turn the corner out of my sight, and for my hands to stop shaking, and then I turned the dial and opened up my locker. The already-ripped corner of the box caught on the edge of the locker door and ripped all the way open, spilling robot parts and sunflower seeds all over the hallway floor. Great.

I opened my backpack and scooped the pieces into it, cramming the power brick down on top of them with a crunch so I could zip the bag closed. Satisfied, I hoisted the backpack onto one shoulder—it weighed a ton now—and headed down the hall, the opposite way that I'd come. Dad would wait for me.

A few seconds later I pushed through the library doors. The librarian smiled and waved at me again.

"Can I help you find something?" she asked.

"Yeah," I said. "I'm wondering if you have any books on how to build robots."

# CHAPTER 8

PROGRAM NAME: The Clog

STEP ONE: Robot moves into brother zone

STEP TWO: Robo-brother is too brothery

STEP THREE: Robot springs leak, rusting his robo-face

Randy and I took so long beating the alien queen in level 19 that I forgot all about the robot until Dad stood in front of the TV to block my view.

"Dad! Move! I've almost got her!" I said, leaning the Ultimate Gaming Zone so far to see around his leg, I almost fell over.

"What's going on? What happened? Why aren't you doing anything?" Randy said in my earpiece.

"You've got a big mess of stuff on the kitchen table," Dad said. "Books, backpack."

"I'll get it later," I said, peering at the tiny piece of screen

I could see between his knees. He squeezed his knees together, forcing me to stop.

"What's happening? Are you still there, Luke? The queen is getting away!" Randy yelled. "Don't let her get away! What are you doing? Talk to me, man! Don't leave me out here alone! They're swarming me, they're swarming!" He started making choking noises, because sometimes Randy could get a little dramatic about our games. I heard the telltale hollow sounds of the game ending. We'd lost.

Exasperated, I let the controller fall into my lap. Dad stayed rooted in his spot. He didn't look pleased, or at all sympathetic to letting the queen get away. "I've been calling for you for half an hour," he said.

"Sorry, I didn't hear you."

"Well, you're hearing me now. Clean up your mess."

"It's not a mess," I argued. "It's important robotics research." Translation: it was highly inconvenient for me to pick it up right now.

Dad glanced behind him at the TV. "Yes, obviously it's very important. Move it. I want it gone before the maws and paws get here."

"Okay, fine," I said. Dad left. "I've gotta go," I said into the microphone.

Randy was still making faint tortured gagging noises, but stopped abruptly. "Oh, okay, dude. No problem. You in trouble?"

"Nah, I just have to work on some stuff."

"Oh, you gotta clean your room?" He started in with the

gagging noises again. Any chore that involved stepping away from the computer made Randy feel like he was going to die.

"No, I have to build a robot."

The gagging noises stopped again. "Dude, you serious?"

"Yeah."

"Does it, like, walk and talk and destroy humanity?"

"No, it just pushes blocks into squares and drives over obstacles and stuff."

"Oh. Still, a robot is cool."

"I guess."

I logged off the game and trudged into the kitchen. I seemed to be doing a lot of trudging lately. Which wasn't entirely normal for me. I mean, I wasn't much of a skipper and nobody ever said, *Hey, that Luke Abbott sure has pep in his step!*, but these days my legs just didn't seem to really want to go along with anything the rest of my body was having to do.

Dad was peeling about a billion potatoes, which must have meant the maws were going to make gnocchi. Dad always started by peeling the potatoes on gnocchi night because the maws would spend so much time arguing over which was the correct way to peel a potato, by the time the gnocchi was made, we would all be in bed for the night.

I wasn't the biggest fan of gnocchi. And after Dad ruined my game, I wasn't the biggest fan of Dad at the moment, either. And then I heard the rumble of Rob's car pulling into the driveway. Great. I definitely wasn't the biggest fan of hanging around when Rob was home.

I took my backpack and books into my bedroom and put them on my bed, then looked around for something to do.

My eyes landed on the robot-building book. It had a photo of a boy in safety goggles tightening a screw on a metal plate. He was wearing kneesocks like the picture of my dad at the skating rink on his ninth birthday.

Surely I could find something more exciting to do.

I cleaned my room. From top to bottom. Which didn't really take that long, because it was Friday, which was the day Dad cleaned the entire house from top to bottom. So I spent a long time straightening my video game cheat-code books and blowing dust off my old Pokémon figures from my serious Pikachu phase.

I looked at the book again. The kid was grinning as if building a robot was the most fun thing he'd ever done in his whole life and he'd just won a big award for Most Positive Robot Builder Ever.

Surely there was something else to clean.

I wandered around in my room for a while longer, until it was obvious that I was officially out of ways to stall and it was time to figure out this robot thing.

I opened my backpack and dumped the parts on the floor. I listlessly picked up a long plastic piece that bent at one end. I rooted around until I found a matching piece and held them up. Together, they looked like smooth plastic claws. Or a gray mustache. I rested them across my top lip and scrunched it up to hold them there.

"Halloo, I'm Mr. Mustache Man," I said. "I love my

mustache. Do you see my mustache? My mustache is monstrous. My mustache is magnificent. Mustache, mustache, mustache."

One of the pieces fell. I picked it up and tucked it inside my top lip so that it stuck down like a tusk. I put the other piece on the other side of my lip to match it. I was a walrus. I spent about five minutes barking and clapping my hands like a seal, because I didn't know what sound walruses made.

So it turned out building a robot wasn't all that bad. I held the pieces on top of my head like antennae and then reenacted the entire science lab scene from *Alien Onslaught*. I found some round pieces and squeezed my eyes around them and then pretended to be surprised by everything I saw. I found a couple of T-shaped pieces and held them at the sides of my neck and walked around Frankenstein-style.

And just as I stuffed two long green pieces up my nostrils and started saying, "What? Is there something hanging out of my nose?" the maws pushed through my door.

We all stared at one another for a moment. One of the green things fell out of my nose and landed with a clatter on the pile of parts. Also, a sunflower seed fell out of my hair. Then the maws sprang into action.

"There's my Lukey-Wukey," Maw Shirley said, coming at me with her pinchy hands.

"Bring those baby cheeks over here," Maw Mazie said.

I pulled the other green piece out of my nose and let it drop onto the pile. "Sorry, maws, not now," I said. "I'm in the middle of something really important."

They exchanged disbelieving glances, so I started randomly rooting through the parts to make it more believable.

"My stars, what is this?" Maw Shirley asked, toeing one of the pieces.

"Looks very technical," Maw Mazie said, bending with a grunt to pick up the book. She held it up and studied the cover. "Well, it's about robots. Are you building a robot, Lukey?"

"Sure am," I said, snapping two pieces together with absolutely no idea what I was going to do with those pieces once I was done. "For school."

"Maybe we should help," Maw Shirley said.

"Oh, good idea! We'll order pizza and forget about the gnocchi."

As much as I loved the idea of pizza over gnocchi, there was no way I was going to let the maws anywhere near my robot.

"That's okay," I said, hurriedly. "I'm going to be working on this all night, probably."

The maws exchanged glances again.

"What? Working on gnocchi night?" Maw Mazie said.

"Your dad's been peeling potatoes for hours," Maw Shirley said.

"Your grandfathers are dying to watch football with you."

I shrugged. "Sorry. It's for school. I can't do anything about it."

Now, you might have thought I'd have felt bad about lying to the maws. After all, they were so sweet, and missing a Friday night meal made by them was one of the worst things they could even think of. But I had no doubt in my mind that if I let the maws help make the robot, it would be an adorable baby robot with very pinchable cheeks and a bottom that would fit into the palms of their hands. And they would figure out a way to make the pieces pink.

I told myself I would eat double portions on the next gnocchi night to make up for the lie.

"There you are." Mom stood in my doorway, pulling an earring off her ear. "Sorry I'm late. I've been looking all over for you two. I think we should have a nice, big salad to go with the gnocchi."

The maws jumped into action, shuffling out of my room, excitedly going on about lettuce and cauliflower and cucumbers and cheese, and completely forgetting about the robot. Mom winked at me over their heads, and then stuck her head into the room after they'd gone.

"Looks like you're really getting into this robotics stuff, huh?" she asked.

"I guess," I said. "I don't really know what I'm doing."

She stepped over the pile of robot parts and kissed my cheek. "You're a very smart boy. I'm sure you'll have it figured out in no time." She pulled the earring off her other ear while she walked to the door. "I'll bring you some gnocchi later," she said over her shoulder.

After Mom left, I decided it was time to really get down to business.

I flipped through the first forty pages of the book, skimming over most of it, and then picked up the same two long pieces and fit them together. I picked up another piece—a flat, black one—and attached it to the side of one. I snapped three more pieces on, and something that rotated. I picked up the power brick and found a spot to stick the whole mess to. I snapped it on, held it up triumphantly, and . . .

Yeah, I wasn't going to be able to do this alone.

I went into Mom and Dad's bedroom and called Walter.

"Hey, Luke, what's up?"

"Remember when you said it sounded like fun to build a robot?"

"Yeah."

I fell back on Mom and Dad's bed. "Does it sound like Friday night fun?"

"Sure. But I can't come over. My cousins are here."

"I'll come there," I said hurriedly. "What time?"

After hanging up with Walter, I went back into the kitchen, expecting to see the maws sweating over cutting boards and pots of boiling water. Instead, the maws were sitting at the kitchen table, drinking coffee and gossiping about someone's unfortunate hair fungus problem, and Dad was the one sweating over the pot of boiling water. Mom was sweating over a cutting board. I heard the paws arguing in the living room.

"Aren't they doing a wonderful job, Lukey-Wukey?" Maw Shirley said.

"Sure," I said. "Hey, um, Dad? I need a ride to Walter's house."

Dad's face was beet red. A sweat bead rolled down his nose and he blotted it with his sleeve. "What? Walter? When?"

"Now."

"Now? No way."

"But I need to go," I said. "It's for school."

"I'm kind of busy here, Luke." As if to punctuate his words, a lid fell off the stove and landed with a clang on the floor. The maws put their hands over their hearts and made startled noises. "Sorry," Dad said.

"Mom? Can you take me?" I asked, but the question quickly dried up in my throat as I saw her harried face over the mountain of lettuce she was chopping. "Never mind," I mumbled.

"You're just going to have to tell Walter you can't come," Dad said.

I thought about the robot parts on my bedroom floor. And the candy at Walter's house. "But I have to go. Can't the maws make dinner like always?"

Dad dropped another lid and muttered under his breath, then wiped his forehead with his sleeve again. "Your grand-mothers are taking a long-overdue break. I am making din-ner tonight, and you're not going to Walter's. There's nobody to take you there. And that is final."

"I can take you."

Rob was standing in the kitchen doorway. I'd been so worried about getting Walter's help with the robot, I'd com-pletely forgotten that the World's Worst Brother was in the house.

"No, thanks," I said, even though saying it broke my rule of never saying anything to Rob ever again for as long as I lived.

"Well, then I guess you're not going," Dad said. "Because Rob is your only way there."

"I'll wait until after dinner," I said.

"I'll be on dish duty then," Dad said. "What about you, Mandy?"

"Clearing the table," Mom said.

"Guess it's Rob or nothing," Dad said. "Take your pick."

I sighed very, very deeply to let Dad know that I knew what he was doing. He was trying to force me to forgive Rob. He was trying to push us back together. Well, it wasn't going to work.

"Fine," I said, then turned to Rob and very icily added, "When are we leaving?"

"Give me five minutes, li'l bro," he said, and jogged out of the room.

I gave my dad my best Are You Happy? look, but he only smiled back like maybe he really was.

I was already waiting in the back seat of Rob's car before he got out there. I figured it would make things less awkward if we weren't walking out to the car at the same time. Plus, I didn't want him to get any ideas that we were friends now. He was my chauffeur. That was how I was going to think about it. I even changed his name, in my head, to Mr. Jeeves, because Mr. Jeeves seemed like a chauffeur-y kind of name.

Soon Rob came out to the car and got in the driver's side.

He fumbled with his keys until he found the right one, and then turned around in his seat.

"You can sit up here, you know," he said.

"No, thank you," I said. *That would be highly inappropriate, Mr. Jeeves,* I added in my head.

He sighed. "Luke. Just come sit up here."

I shook my head, staring straight ahead, as if I didn't even see him. I started to feel that familiar clog in my throat—the one I always got before I was about to cry. Or throw up. Sometimes it was hard to tell if it was tears or barf that was going to pour out of my face until it was actually happening.

I remembered three summers ago, when Rob and I built a fort in the woods behind our house. Nobody knew we were doing it—not even Mom and Dad. It was our secret. We'd drag scraps of wood and old pizza boxes and broken cinder blocks and anything else we could find out into the trees and would arrange them, day by day, into a house structure. Rob even borrowed some of Dad's tools so we could hammer things together, and I borrowed an old bath rug from the hall closet so we could lie down inside our fort without getting bugs on our shirts. By the end of the summer, we had a two-room fort, with windows and everything, and we would play Fort Invaders, a made-up game where we pretended we were holding enemy troops at bay and saving our town. I was always the lookout, up in a tree, and would scramble down about every five minutes screaming, "They're coming! They're coming! Arm yourselves, men!"

Sometimes we would just sit in the fort and talk. Rob

would mostly talk about girls, who seemed to be a constant source of misery for him, and I would pretend that I understood his torment, even though I couldn't figure out for the life of me why he would want anything to do with girls in the first place. And every now and then we would talk about Mom and Dad, and about how sometimes other people acted like it was weird that Dad stayed home with us and did all the chores while Mom went to a job every day, but how we didn't understand why anyone worried about that, because it was the way it had always been in our house and it wasn't any big deal. And sometimes we would just tell a whole lot of fart jokes.

That summer was the best summer of my life. I wanted it to never end.

It did. And so did the summer after that and the summer after that, and now there would be no more summers, because Rob was going to spend this summer in boot camp and then he would go away and by the time the marines let him come back home, he wouldn't be coming to our home at all.

It was like every summer was ending, and he thought it would somehow all be okay if I just sat in the front seat with him.

"Come on, Luke. I'm not going to drive until you move up here."

I reached for the door handle. "Then I'll walk," I said, even though I had no idea how to get to Walter's house because it was all the way on the other side of town.

Rob grunted and twisted the key. The car roared to

life. "Fine. Have your way." He backed out of the driveway, and I accidentally let my eye catch his. "You can't stay mad at me forever, you know."

I swallowed. The clog in my throat started to hurt, which meant soon I wouldn't be able to talk without getting that embarrassing cry-wobble in my voice. "Watch me," I said, satisfied that I still sounded kind of steely.

He gazed at me a moment longer, and then reluctantly put the car into drive. "I'm sorry that I've disappointed you, but you have to know that my joining the marines isn't about you," he said to the windshield. "It's just something that's important to me. Remember all those games of Fort Invaders we used to play? Remember what I always used to say?"

I did. *Man, I can't wait until I grow up*, he used to say, sitting with his back propped against the outside wall of the fort, catching his breath. *I'm going to be a real soldier then*. It was something Rob had always wanted to do. I just had never thought he'd actually go and do it.

"I had to grow up, li'l bro. You will, too," he said.

I didn't answer. The clog wouldn't let me.

# CHAPTER 9

PROGRAM NAME: Helping Hand
STEP ONE: Robot is pathetic
STEP TWO: Robot visits nonpathetic robot
   friend who knows what a chassis is
STEP THREE: Both robots dance samba

For some reason, they were having a fiesta at Walter's house. An actual fiesta, with yellow and orange flags hanging from the living room doorway, refried beans on the stove, and a piñata in the garage. Cousins were racing everywhere, one of them with a giant floppy sombrero on his head.

"*¡Hola!*" Walter cried when he opened the door to let me in. Mariachi music tumbled out from behind him.

"What's—?"

He grabbed my shoulder and tugged. "Come in, come in! The tamales will be ready in half an hour." I stumbled inside and he took the bag full of robot parts from me. He peered inside. "Oh, yeah, we should have that mostly knocked out in half an hour. Then we can join the samba contest."

"Half an hour? Samba what?" I asked, trailing behind him.

We skirted a few cousins, stole two sopapillas from a wandering aunt, and ended up in Walter's bedroom. He shut the door behind us, muffling the music.

"Okay, let's get started," he said. He dumped the plastic bag of parts onto the floor and sank down onto his knees next to them. "You have the book?"

I pulled the book from my backpack and handed it to him. He opened it up and immediately began reading through it, nodding his head every so often as if it made total sense to him.

"Uh, Walter?" I asked, unsure what to do with myself while he read.

"Huh?" He didn't look up.

"Why are you having a fiesta?" I asked.

He shrugged, still not looking up. "Because it's Friday," he said. "And we had the Oktoberfest last weekend."

"Oktoberfest?"

He laid the book at his side and began sifting through the parts. "You know, Wiener schnitzel, spaetzle, that kind of thing."

"What the heck is a winger spatula?"

He giggled and blew a curl out of his eye. "Not winger spatula. Wiener schnitzel. It's a traditional German veal dish."

"Are you German?"

He looked at me as if I'd just asked the most ridiculous

question he'd ever heard. "Of course not," he said, and that seemed to be the explanation for everything. Walter's family was having a fiesta because they'd already had Oktoberfest, and they'd had Oktoberfest because of course they're not German. Made perfect sense in Walterville.

I rested my hands on my thighs and leaned forward, picking through the pieces. "So you think you can help with this?"

He rolled his eyes. "I've built most of an MK4 Roadster kit car with my uncle. I think a little robot will be no problem."

"Should we get your uncle?"

"Nah," he said. "He's making salsa right now. I think I've got this."

I watched as Walter expertly snapped pieces into place, the power brick becoming a car; the car becoming a truck; the truck becoming a . . . robot. He bounced in place as songs changed in the depths of the house. A couple of times he hummed along, as if he'd been listening to fiesta music all his life.

"Walter?" I finally asked, when he looked like he was nearly done.

"Yep?" He snapped a hook onto the back of the bot.

"Does it need a chassis?"

Again he stopped and gave me the incredulous look. "Why would it need a chassis?" he asked.

I let out a breath. "I don't know. I'm still trying to figure out if a chassis is food. Are we eating a chassis tonight?"

He laughed, a holding-his-belly, rocking-backward-so-I-could-see-his-tonsils kind of laugh. "You are so funny, Luke

Abbott," he said once he got a hold of himself. "For a second there I thought you were serious."

I had been serious. But Walter didn't need to know that. I held my belly and rocked backward, too, forcing out a laugh to match his.

He worked for a few more minutes and then held up the bot.

"Ta-da!" he cheered.

I gazed at the robot. It looked like an actual robot. It had four big rough-tread wheels, a hook sticking out from one end, and the two pieces I'd had jammed up my nostrils just hours before sticking out of the other end. Wires snaked around the side of it, and when Walter pushed a button on top, the pieces I'd had jammed up my nose slowly closed like a crab's claw.

He turned the bot over. "This right here is a color sensor," he said. His finger trailed wires that snaked up the robot's side. "It will sense color changes and will follow a trail of color. So you can program it to follow a line, and it won't ever get off course. It also has a sensor on the front here." He turned the bot around and showed me what looked like a little camera. "That senses when the bot is getting close to an object and will make it stop before it knocks into anything it shouldn't. Somewhere you should have a gyroscope, but I don't see it here."

He looked at me expectantly, and I shrugged. Maybe the gyroscope was the thing that had skittered out of my locker and across the hallway floor, landing behind the trash can and I was too afraid of what might be behind a middle school trash can to go after it.

"Well, if you find the gyroscope, you can attach it, too. It will help your bot orient itself." He assessed the robot fondly. "Basically what you have here is a very sweet piece of complex machinery. It can do anything from pick up objects to knock stuff down to turn circles in a victory dance. Not too shabby, huh?"

I nodded, not because I'd understood anything he'd just said, but because he'd looked so triumphant while he'd said it.

"Walter," I said, "you really should be on the team. You're good at building stuff. You want me to ask Mr. Terry about getting you on it? You can have my spot!" Which sounded really generous, but was actually just me trying to replace myself so I no longer had to be on the team.

"Nah," he said, getting up and brushing off the front of his jeans. He started dancing in place. "I've got cars to build. Did you know that the Mastretta MXT is Mexico's premiere sports car? It's got more than 240 horsepower and can reach over 140 miles per hour."

I shook my head. "Nope."

"If that isn't reason to have a fiesta, I don't know what is!" he cried. He flung open his bedroom door, and music and laughter flooded in. Two cousins spilled by, giggling and flinging balloons at each other.

"Ooh! Balloon fight!" Walter cried. He disappeared into the party.

It definitely wasn't any quieter than having the maws and paws around, but the tamales smelled delicious and the music was pretty great and there were cousins with balloons.

I jumped into the balloon fight after him.

# CHAPTER 10

PROGRAM NAME: Self-Destruction
STEP ONE: Robot is minding his own
    business
STEP TWO: Girl robots appear with
    sparkles and hair accessories
STEP THREE: Now-sparkly robot hides in
    corner, hoping his battery will die

I knew it wasn't going to be good news when Missy the Cruel stood over the robot for a solid ten minutes without saying anything. I pushed the same button Walter had pushed at his house, and waited for the pincers to close. Instead, a loud buzz emitted from the power brick and the robot shivered and then did nothing. Clearly, the robot just didn't like me.

"That's the ugliest robot I've ever seen," Missy said. "I should have known you'd mess it up. Why did we let Loser Luke get his loser hands on it, anyway?" she asked the group at large. "We'll never win anything now."

"I think it's kind of cute," Mikayla said. She pointed at the hook with her big toe. "We could put some rhinestones on the tail here."

"It's not a tail," I said. "It's a hook."

"For—" one Jacob said.

"What?" the other Jacob finished. I cringed. I hated it when they shared a two-word sentence. It really seemed unnecessary. And creepy.

"For . . . hooking things," I said.

"Like . . . ?" Stuart prodded. He popped a sunflower seed into his mouth.

"Like . . . things," I said. "I don't know. Things that need hooks to hook them. I'm sure something will need to be hooked."

"Well, that just seems really dumb," Missy the Cruel said. "It figures that you can't even tell us what the parts are for. I say we tear it apart and start over." She reached for the robot.

"No," I said, lunging forward and grabbing it before she could get her miniature hands on it. Even though I hadn't technically been the one to build it, I still felt kind of protective of the robot. It had sat on my dresser all weekend and stared at me with its two eye stalks. Or whatever those things were Walter had put on the top of it that looked like eye stalks. It kind of felt like a pet now.

"Why should you get the only say?" Stuart said. He crunched a sunflower seed. "It's not your robot. We're a team. I'm with Missy. I say we should start over."

"Maybe we could just tie some yarn to its nose," Mikayla suggested. "I can tie bows with my toes, did you know that?"

"Everyone in the world knows that," I said. "And it's not a nose. It's a gripper. And it doesn't need bows."

"A gripper?" Missy said incredulously. "That doesn't sound very technical."

"Well, it grips things, doesn't it?" I asked.

"I think you're looking for the word 'claw,' " Jacob said.

"I don't know," the other Jacob said. "It's not really very clawlike. It's only got two pieces. A claw should have at least three, don't you think?"

"Good point, Jacob."

"Thank you, Jacob."

"They're *forceps*," Missy interjected. "If you were paying attention in vocab at all, instead of eating glue, you would know that."

"I don't know, they look more like tongs to me," Stuart said. He mimicked a tonging motion with his hands.

"I can work salad tongs with my toes," Mikayla said.

"We know," we all said in unison.

All except one person, of course. The one person hanging out in the back of the room in his camouflage jacket not saying anything to anyone. Lunchbox Jones. I chanced a peek to see if he was still awake. He was, but he had his head down, his chin resting on his lunchbox. He was watching us silently.

His eyes met mine. I looked away quickly.

"Right," Missy said matter-of-factly. "Time to say good-bye to Loser Luke's lame design." I had been so rattled by meeting Lunchbox's gaze, I was too slow to react. Before I could even reach out, Missy had snatched up the robot and had begun taking off the parts that Walter had put on.

"No," I said, reaching for it. "Not the eye stalks! At least leave the eye stalks!"

But Missy didn't listen to me. Of course. Missy never listened to anyone but herself. Soon she was holding just the power brick. Mikayla was fashioning rhinestones that she seemed to produce out of nowhere onto some large, flat pieces. The Jacobs rolled a wheel back and forth between each other, every so often cheering over points gained in a secret game only they understood. And Stuart was using the color sensor cable to dislodge a sunflower shell out from between two molars. I sat heavily at my Life Skills desk.

Why bother? All the work I had put in—okay, all the work Walter had put in—was undone. Missy would never let me have a say. Let her win.

I glanced up at the ceiling tile above Evan Miller's desk, the one with all the pencils stuck in it.

Well, if I couldn't win with the robot, at least I could gain some kind of victory. I leaned over and rooted around in my backpack until I found the pencil stub I'd been using for the past week. It was so short I had to contort my hand to write with it. It had teeth marks in it—which was somewhat unsettling since I hated the taste of pencils and never chewed mine—and the eraser was flat and slick.

The perfect pencil to retire.

I got up and gave it one last shaving, almost losing it in the sharpener. Then took it back to my desk and lined up the perfect shot. I could have gotten closer—say, Amber Watts's desk, which had a much straighter path than mine—but that would have been an unfair advantage, and thus cheating according to the unofficial rules of the unofficial official game of Pencil Stick. Plus, throwing from my desk, there was always a chance that I would miss. And since Missy the Cruel was standing directly on the other side of Evan's desk, my pencil might possibly fall and land right on the top of her head. Bonus.

I decided to go with a traditional paper airplane throw method, winding up and giving a few practice aims. Satisfied with my trajectory, I pulled my arm back and let loose. My pencil stub sailed through the air and found its home—right smack in the center of the ceiling tile. I threw my arms up in victory just as Missy turned.

"And another thing, Loser Luke Abbott," she said, holding the robot. Her eyes traveled up to the ceiling tile, grew round, and then narrowed into two slits again as she looked at me. A grin crept up one side of her mouth. "Never mind," she said mildly.

This was bad. Very, very bad. There was no way Missy Farnham was going to let me get away with this.

I sat at my desk and wondered about all the ways I could get in trouble for defiling school property.

I imagined myself being a high school outcast. *That's Luke Abbott. You know, the guy who vandalized the middle school? We should stay far away from him. Protect our reputations.*

I imagined myself being kept in a special dorm in college.

*Here you go, Mr. Abbott. Your room is on the left—the one with no ceilings. We call this the defiling delinquents' wing.*

I imagined myself trying to get a job and being turned away. *I'm sorry, Mr. Abbott, but we have ceilings at this business, and your record clearly indicates that you can't be trusted with those.*

I imagined myself shelving library books and washing beakers in the chemistry wing as punishment until I was forty. *Happy fortieth birthday, Mr. Abbott. You've worked off approximately one-sixteenth of your ceiling debt with us.*

I really needed to stop imagining things.

After a few minutes, Mr. Terry came into the room. "Hello, team," he said. "Good to see you're all here. I have some things to show you. How's the robot coming?"

Mikayla held up a part with each foot. They sparkled. "We're beautifying," she said.

"It's just about finished," Missy added. She snapped two more pieces in place. "There. That should do it." She held up the robot. It looked pretty much exactly like it had looked before.

"Much—"

"Better," the Jacobs added.

"Are you kidding me? It looks just like it did when I brought it in," I said. "You're such a cheat—"

Missy glared at me and then flicked her eyes up toward the ceiling tile. "Looks great, Missy," I mumbled.

"That's the spirit!" Mr. Terry said. "I like to see the team working together. And so will the judges when we go to competition. Being good sports is very important in robotics. Can't win without it."

Oh, great. We wouldn't win unless Missy Farnham was a good sport? We would never win. Which, I guessed, wasn't a totally bad thing. We were Forest Shade Middle School, after all.

"Come on," Mr. Terry said. "I need to show you something."

We followed him out of the classroom, Missy walking right next to him and carrying the robot. I lingered in the back, but not too far back, because I could feel Lunchbox Jones's ox breath behind me, could hear the squeak of his lunchbox swinging back and forth on its handle.

"Where are we going?" one of the Jacobs whispered to the other.

"I was going to ask the same thing," the other Jacob responded.

Mr. Terry led us through the empty cafeteria, where the custodian was polishing the floor, down the sixth grade hallway, and into the industrial tech room. Back in one corner was a large rectangular table standing on two sawhorses. Mr. Terry went to the table and ran his hand along one edge.

"This is our competition table," he said. He pulled a big roll of canvas out of a nearby cardboard box, stood at one end of the table, and unrolled the canvas, which perfectly fit the dimensions of the table. "And this," he said, slightly out of breath, "is our mat."

We all leaned over the table and took a look. The mat

was covered with lines and pictures and squares made out of dotted lines, kind of like a map.

"We'll put the obstacles in these squares," he said. "And the robot will maneuver over the table completing tasks around those obstacles."

Stuart gazed at the robot, then back at the table, and then at the robot again. "How will it know what to do?" he asked.

"We'll program it using that computer over there," Mr. Terry said, gesturing to a laptop on a desk near the industrial tech teacher's office.

"*We'll* program it?" Stuart asked. "*Us?* Does anybody here know how to program a robot?"

"Not exactly," Mr. Terry said, scratching his neck uneasily. "But it can't be too hard for a bunch of young people such as yourselves to figure out. I guess."

"You mean even *you* don't know how?" Mikayla asked. "So nobody can do it?"

We all looked at one another, each of us shrugging, except for Missy, who shrugged at everyone else but glared at me. And Lunchbox, whom nobody would make eye contact with, but who had nothing to say, anyway.

"Huh," Mr. Terry finally said. "Looks like we'll have a bit of a learning curve ahead of us, then. I thought maybe since some of you were big video game players . . ."

He directed his gaze at me, but I pretended to be really interested in the state of the toe of my shoe at that particular moment.

"Luke?" he prodded.

I turned up my palms in defeat. "I know how to beat them, not program them."

Missy made a noise. "Figures," she said. "You know what else Luke knows, Mr. Terry? He definitely knows how to stick pencils in the ceiling tiles in the classrooms. He threw one in yours today."

Mr. Terry looked weary. "Thank you, Missy," he said. "Let's go back to the classroom."

# CHAPTER 11

PROGRAM NAME: Sink Terror
STEP ONE: Robot needs refreshing
STEP TWO: Robot stumbles upon terror at
   bathroom sink
STEP THREE: Robot races away, shrieking

I didn't get in trouble for the ceiling tile. I'd braced myself for it and had slunk around the school for days, jumping half out of my skin every time I saw Principal McMillan coming my way. Once I nearly walked right into him rounding a corner in the hallway and actually screamed out loud.

When we got to Life Skills class Tuesday, however, the ceiling tile above Evan Miller's desk was empty, except for a whole lot of holes. Mr. Terry's desk also sported a new pencil cup that was brimming with sharpened pencils. My stub pencil wasn't there. I felt sad that it had gone from being the centerpiece of the beautiful ceiling tile, there for everyone to admire and appreciate, to most likely being in the Dumpster behind the field house. Also, since nobody but Missy had witnessed it, I had no proof that I had actually gotten it up there. And people were not given to just taking other people's word for it when it came to Pencil Stick.

But at least I never got in trouble for it. Mr. Terry must have figured he had bigger things to worry about than the ceiling tile, and he couldn't afford to lose a robotics team member, even though that member knew absolutely nothing about how to program a robot.

Plus everyone was really mad at Missy for tattling. Which would have been awesome had she not been absent from school for the whole rest of the week. It wasn't very fun to be mad at someone who wasn't there to know you were mad at them.

But we were mad, especially those of us with the highest Pencil Stick scores to uphold, and most of our time that week was spent pondering the ways we could get back at Missy Farnham for what she did. I voted strongly for a jump-rope song, which I was still trying to formulate:

*Missy, Missy, she's a sissy.*

*She does things that are really fishy.*

*And her underwear are crispy.*

*And she eats rocks.*

It was still a work in progress. Also, I was starting to understand why I didn't do very well in the poetry unit last year.

And when we weren't talking about revenge on Missy,

we were trying to decide when would be a good time to start the Pencil Stick game over. Would Mr. Terry be more likely to notice, now that he knew it had happened the first time? Or would he assume we would be too scared to start the game over and so be less likely to notice? Maybe if we started the game over on a different ceiling tile he wouldn't notice? Or maybe we should try another class? Maybe Señora Vasquez's Spanish class. She noticed everything, which would definitely give the game higher stakes.

By the time Friday got here, I was so exhausted from all the thinking and planning, I wasn't sure how I'd ever make it through another round of football in gym class.

"I've got licorice," Walter said when I got to his locker. He twirled a licorice whip in front of my nose.

"Nah," I said. "Thanks, anyway." I moved around him to my locker.

The licorice whip swung around once more and then just hung there. Walter looked stunned. "You don't want any?" he asked. His voice was soft and wary, like they do in the movies when they have to defuse a bomb and they aren't sure if they should cut the blue wire or the red wire and suddenly the guy doing the cutting realizes that he's colorblind, anyway. "What does this mean?" I heard him ask under his breath.

I opened the locker. The empty beat-up robot box mocked me from inside. I kicked it for good measure, shoved my whole backpack into the locker, and shut the door.

"I'm not very hungry," I said.

"Okay," Walter said in a way that sounded anything but

actually okay. "We'll just . . . walk, then? I guess? Can we do that?"

"Sure." But I found myself walking very slowly.

"So my uncle and I put on the sunroof last night," Walter said. "Actually, the hardest part was using the sheet metal shear. Well, that's not exactly true. The hardest part was getting my mom to let us use a sheet metal shear, because she was worried that I'd cut off my whole arm or my head or something. But my uncle talked her into it, because he's the big brother and says he has his ways of making her remember that, and once we got started"—he made two zipping sounds and swished his hands around—"we were done! Easy peasy! And"—he flailed his arm around dramatically and rolled his head on his neck—"arm and head intact. Awesome, right?"

"Sure," I said. But it was obvious I wasn't into it, even more than usual. I wondered if maybe I should splash some cold water on my face to wake up a little.

"You sure you don't want some licorice?" he asked, swinging it at me again.

"Yeah, I actually think I'm going to stop in the restroom on my way to the gym. I'll catch you at lunch, okay?"

Walter looked really uncertain now. Maybe even a little scared. "Okay. Sure, Luke. No problem. See you then."

I ducked into the boys' room that nobody ever used back in the corner by the guidance office before he could ask any more questions, like if I was okay or if I needed anything or another one of those questions that grown-ups were always asking. Walter was kind of like a grown-up in a kid's body, so it wouldn't surprise me if he started saying grown-up things. *Bless your heart, Luke, you let me know if there's anything I can do.* But that didn't mean I wanted to answer those kinds of questions.

Mostly because I couldn't. I mean, was there anything wrong with me? I didn't know. Seemed like maybe a lot of things were wrong, but I wasn't used to a lot of things being wrong in my life. I was exhausted. I was still mad about my last conversation with Rob. I was dreading Friday night with the maws and paws. And I was stuck on the robotics team with Missy the Cruel and Lunchb—

I wasn't paying attention as I plowed into the bathroom and almost bumped headfirst right into Lunchbox Jones. The bell rang at that very moment, which made me jump about a foot and maybe even scream a little.

Lunchbox was hovered over the bathroom sink. His face was dripping and his hair was wet around the edges. He'd taken off his camouflage jacket and hung it over the radiator, and—weirdest of all—his lunchbox was perched on top of it.

He froze, bent over the sink, staring at me in the mirror. His eyes went wide. I froze, one foot still raised like I was going to take a step. My eyes went wider.

Suddenly he grabbed his lunchbox and clutched it to his chest, like he was afraid I was going to steal it. He snarled, showing all his teeth. I hopped three steps backward, bumping into the door.

"What are you looking at?" he growled. Only it sounded like:

# WHAT ARE YOU LOOKING AT?!?!

(with lion roars echoing off the bathroom walls and antelopes being chased out of bushes and stuff).

I opened my mouth and tried to assure him that I wasn't actually looking at anything, even though I was totally looking at him. I mean, who wouldn't, right? He wasn't wearing his jacket. He was washing his face in the sink. He wasn't holding his lunchbox . . . and then he was holding it like it was a baby. I wasn't the smartest guy at Forest Shade Middle School, but even I understood that something weird was going on here.

But nothing would come out of my mouth. Still, the only appropriate answer that anyone should ever give Lunchbox Jones when he asks what you're looking at should be "nothing," and if you can't say the word "nothing," just do what I did.

I shook my head so hard my ears rang.

And then I turned and tried to push my way through the pull door. And I may have walked directly into the door a few times before my brain fired off the right door-opening protocol, which, in this case, meant I had to talk my feet into moving backward toward Lunchbox a few steps so I could pull the door open.

Once I finally got it right, I lunged out into the hallway and ran all the way to the gym, across the gym floor and to my locker. I was moving so fast, I actually got there before the tardy bell rang.

I pressed my back to the cool locker and bent over, my hands on my knees, sucking in breath. I closed my eyes and watched little lights dance in front of my eyelids. One thing was for sure—I was wide awake now. So much adrenaline coursed through me I might never sleep again.

I was still dressing when everyone else filed out to our squad lines.

Which gave me time to calm down, and once I was calm, I started to think.

What was Lunchbox doing in the restroom, anyway? Why was he washing up at school first thing in the morning? And, more importantly, what was in that lunchbox that was so important?

# CHAPTER 12

```
PROGRAM NAME: Corned Beef Hash
STEP ONE: Robot innocently rolls into
    kitchen area
STEP TWO: Robot smells something awful
STEP THREE: Robot tips over on side and
    plays dead
```

The maws and paws were already at my house by the time Dad and I got home. According to Dad, they'd been there since mid afternoon, working on a corned beef hash recipe that the maws couldn't agree on for anything. They finally agreed to make dual corned beef hash dishes and let the family decide which one tasted the best. A corned beef hash showdown.

I hated corned beef hash. The idea of taste-testing two of them made me want to go back to school and just wait out the weekend.

"So how's robotics going?" Dad asked on the way home. "You don't seem to really talk about it."

I shrugged. "It's okay," I said, mostly because I didn't like to talk about it at all, but also because it seemed really important to Dad that I enjoy robotics, and I didn't want to hurt his feelings by telling him I would rather be playing *Alien Onslaught* with Randy. We'd left the game at the brink of beating level 21 the night before. It killed me that the paws had most definitely already claimed the TV and Randy would beat the level without me. Randy was great at reenacting what had happened while I was gone, complete with mouth-clicky alien noises, but it was never as good as the real thing.

"I never got to tell you how cool I thought the robot looked. You did a great job with it."

"Walter did it, really," I said. "Plus, the team rebuilt it after. I didn't have anything to do with it. But thanks."

"Don't sell yourself short, Luke. You may not have put the pieces on the robot, but that doesn't necessarily mean you had nothing to do with it. You've got talent you don't even know about. You'll see."

He pulled into the driveway, and the moment we opened the car doors, we could hear the maws bickering from inside the house. Dad sighed. "They get worse every week, don't they?" he asked.

I nodded and rubbed my cheek absently. He had no idea.

"Sorry, bud, your mom won't be home for another couple hours. Prepare to be pinched."

Apparently dads weren't as dedicated to saving you from overbearing grandma love as moms were. Or at least my dad wasn't.

The maws met me at the door, each with a spoon in her hand.

"There he is! Try this, Lukey-Wukey, and tell me it isn't the best hash you've ever tasted." Maw Shirley simultaneously crammed a mouthful of hash into my face and pinched my cheek so hard it nearly mushed the food right back out of my mouth.

"Don't you listen to her. She used canned corned beef. Canned, can you believe it? Here, try this one. It's the only hash you'll ever need to eat for the rest of your life."

*I hope that's true,* I thought as another spoonful of the most awful food ever invented was shoved into my mouth. As I chewed, my other cheek was squeezed within an inch of its life.

They stood in front of me, each holding her empty spoon against her chest, smiling hopefully.

"Mmmm," I said, nodding. I tried to get around them, but they inched to their left, keeping me trapped.

"Well?" they said together.

"You won't hurt her feelings. Tell her mine is the best. Canned corned beef, mind you," Maw Mazie said.

"No, no, you don't have to lie to protect your old granny there. She understands her hash could never touch mine."

I wished the hash had never touched me. My stomach gurgled into what I was pretty sure was Emergency Mode.

"Yum, is that corned beef hash I smell?" Rob said, coming into the kitchen. He patted his stomach with both hands, smiling wide at the maws. "When's it gonna be ready? I'm starved!"

The maws forgot all about me and went back to their pots, the argument starting anew.

"Try mine first. You'll see she doesn't know the first thing about corned beef hash," Maw Shirley said.

"I know enough not to use canned corned beef. Come over here, Robby Wobby. Let me get at those cheeks."

I could hardly believe it. Rob hated corned beef hash as much as I did. I knew this for a fact. Once we stole the leftovers and threw them down the storm sewer so Mom would quit making us eat them. Had Rob changed so much he now even liked corned beef hash? Traitor!

He followed the maws over to their pots, cheeks out. He eagerly gobbled up spoonfuls of corned beef hash and told them both that hers was the best and said he couldn't wait for more.

I stared hard at him, looking for a telltale sign that he was lying. But there was none.

Instead, I saved myself, bolting for my bedroom the minute the maws' backs were turned.

"Hey-hey-hey," Dad said, grabbing my sleeve before I could get to the stairs. "You need to go in there and say hello to the paws. You missed them last week while you were at Walter's, remember?"

"Okay," I said. I dropped my backpack on the bottom step. This would take a while.

The paws were watching bowling.

"Did you see that? I think his toe went over the line! Line foul! Line foul!" Paw Stanley cried, reaching for his imaginary coach's whistle.

Paw Morris belly laughed. "Oh-ho! Beautiful spin on that ball! Just beautiful! I could get you a deal on a good bowling ball, you know."

I came in and flopped in Dad's recliner. A bowler got a strike, and both paws came up off the couch as if the guy had just scored a Super Bowl–winning touchdown.

"Wow! What a game! What a guy!"

"Did you see that? Did you see it?"

"I saw it! I saw— Hey, look who's here!"

Both paws crowded around the recliner. "Well, it's a long-lost stranger. So glad you could join us for a change."

I smiled and nodded, acted like it was all big fun when what I really wanted to do was go into my bedroom and be alone. Or turn the TV to *Alien Onslaught* and help save Randy from the blue-faced nose-eating aliens.

"Where were you last Friday night? Have a date?" Paw Stanley asked.

Paw Morris wiggled his bushy eyebrows up and down. "You bet he did. Is she cute? What's her name?"

"Walter," I said.

They glanced at each other, confused.

"Walter's kind of an ugly name for a girl," Paw Morris said. "I guess she could shorten it, though? Wallina?"

Paw Stanley shook his head. "Wallina isn't short for Walter. Maybe just Wally?"

"Still sounds pretty masculine," Paw Morris said.

"Walter isn't a girl. I wasn't with a girl," I said. "I was with my friend, Walter. Who is a boy. He builds cars."

"And robots," Dad interjected as he came into the room, wiping his hands on a towel. "It's hopeless in there," he said, pointing toward the kitchen with his thumb. "They're arguing over onion size now."

"Makes a difference in flavor," Paw Morris said sagely.

"Luke tell you why he wasn't here last Friday?" Dad asked. He tucked the towel into his waistband. Dad always had a towel tucked in his waistband. He said it was a habit he started when Rob was a baby and was always barfing on stuff.

"Well," Paw Stanley said, "so far all we can get out of him is he has a girlfriend named Walter."

I closed my eyes and held my forehead in my palm. Sometimes it was as if the paws were trying not to get it.

"Oh! Spare!" Paw Morris said, pointing at the TV.

"Walter is his friend. A boy," Dad said, sounding just like me. "And Luke went over to build a robot for his robotics team. It's really something. Has grippers and wheels and hooks and wires. Like nothing you've seen before."

"I thought he was playing football," Paw Stanley said. "I thought we'd settled that."

"Nope. Luke's a robotics guy," Dad said. He tapped his temple. "He understands all this computer gobbledygook us old farts don't get."

"Well, I don't exactly get it, either," I said, but nobody was really listening to me. The paws were half arguing and half bemoaning a bowler missing a split, and the maws seemed to have ramped up their argument in the kitchen again.

Soon the noise spilled Rob out into the living room. He held his stomach. He looked green. He belched. Three times. On the third time, Dad jumped out of the way and scrambled for the towel on his belt.

"Corned beef hash," Rob muttered miserably, falling limply into a chair. "Corned beef hash." He belched again and made a terrible face. His eyes roamed to meet mine, and in that moment I understood. He still hated the stuff. Maybe he hadn't changed into a totally different person.

We locked eyes. Rob's seemed to be begging for forgiveness.

"You get used to that hash, soldier," Paw Morris said. "You'll be eating a lot worse in the service." He and Paw Stanley elbowed each other, laughing. Dad joined in, tousling Rob's hair, and soon Rob was laughing, too.

"After a day in boot camp, I'll probably be glad to eat anything they'll give me," Rob said. "I heard we'll march for ten hours straight."

"Is that right?" Paw Morris asked.

Paw Stanley nodded. "But it'll seem like twenty."

"They're gonna wean you off that junk food, make you a muscle man," Paw Morris added.

Rob flexed his arms and grinned. "I am ready for it, sir!" he growled.

And just like that, I didn't want to forgive him, no matter how much corned beef hash he ate.

# CHAPTER 13

PROGRAM NAME: Mad Bot
STEP ONE: Bot doesn't feel like being
 programmed
STEP TWO: Bot crosses arm attachments
 and refuses to cooperate
STEP THREE: Bot gets angry and goes all
 tirade crazy

We spent the first twenty minutes of practice staring at a blank computer screen and quietly arguing over who would have to sit down and try to make the first run at programming the robot. Mr. Terry had left to take a phone call, telling us to "get a feel for the program." So far all we'd felt was certainty that one of us was going to break the computer or the robot or both.

"You do it," Mikayla said, nudging me forward.

"No way," I said. "You do it. Can't you type like a million words a minute with your toes?"

She gave a haughty look. "This isn't a typing test. And it's ninety-two, thank you. Eighty-nine if I'm wearing socks."

I turned to the Jacobs. They stepped back, holding their palms out. "Don't look at us," they said in unison.

"We're only here because our moms wanted us to join a team," one of them said.

"And we didn't think we'd be as good at football as the guinea pig," the other added.

I tried Stuart, but he was too busy stuffing his hands into his jacket pockets, talking to himself. "I'm out?" he said in a panicky voice. "I ate them all? Can't be."

I turned the other direction, but the only person over there was Lunchbox, and I wasn't about to ask him a thing. Especially not after seeing him in the bathroom.

Where was Missy when you needed her? She was still gone, which was weird, and I half wondered if someone had gotten revenge on her, after all. Normally she would have been the first one to jump up and declare herself an expert, no matter if she had no clue how to do whatever it was she was claiming to be an expert at. She would have pushed me out of the way to get to the computer before I could. I would have been more than happy to let her expertly program the robot that "she" made. But she was gone and the Jacobs were trying on hard hats and Stuart was having a silent empty-mouthed meltdown and Mikayla was painting her toenails, and somebody had to do something.

"Fine," I said. "I'll do it. Get me the robot."

I pulled up the program and tried to make sense of it. There were boxes lined up along the bottom of the screen, with symbols that made no sense, percentages and numbers and words like "loop interrupt." The rest of the screen was mostly blank, waiting for me to start telling it to do things.

Carefully, I clicked on a box. It followed my mouse. So far, so good. I had no idea what the box did, but I dragged it up into the middle of the screen, clicked a few settings, and left it there. I went back down to the bottom of the screen and clicked another box. A different kind, because . . . well, I had no idea why. I clicked some different numbers on that one, and rotated a symbol.

I sat back and admired the work. It looked complicated. Technical. Yet it was only about dragging and clicking things. It was actually quite easy. If this was all it took to program robots, I was going to be a rocket scientist before I got to high school.

"Are you sure you know what you're doing?" Mikayla asked, peering over my shoulder. "What does 'medium motor' mean?"

"Of course I'm sure. What do you think medium motor means? It means it's not large or small, right? Our robot looks pretty medium to me."

She chewed her lip as she gazed at the robot, which sat on the mat nearby. "I don't know. I mean, some robots are really, really huge, right? So this one would be very small in comparison. But then other robots might be tiny. Like you can't even see them with your naked eye."

The two Jacobs nudged each other and giggled. "She just said 'naked.'"

Mikayla made a face at them, then turned back to me

and continued. "As I was saying, some robots out there could be the size of . . ." She looked around. Stuart had sunk into a chair and was hugging himself. "A sunflower seed," she said. "Compared to that robot, our robot would be huge. It's really unfair to judge a robot on its size. When my mom and I went shopping for the winter dance last year, some of the dresses I wore said they were larges, but they were so not larges. I could barely get my big toe in them."

"We're not judging the robot," I said. "And we're not buying dresses. For robots or for toes. Do you mind?"

"Okay, fine. But I'm just saying. That robot could be an extra small and you're making it feel bad about itself because you're calling it a medium."

As mad as I'd been at Rob, I was instantly glad—and not for the first time—that I did not have any sisters.

"Fine. Here." I pulled a "small motor" box out of the bottom line-up and dragged it up next to the others. I clicked a few things and gave her a smug look. "Happy?"

"Who said it was a small?" she asked.

I grunted and pulled a "large motor" box up with the others. "There," I said. "Done. Now it is every size." In the back of my head, it seemed kind of impossible that one thing could be every size, but I was willing to say or do just about anything to make Mikayla stop talking at that point.

Fortunately, it worked. She sauntered away to where the Jacobs were. "I can use a hammer with my feet, did you know that?" I heard her ask, and soon I heard the sound of hammer meeting wood on the other side of the room.

But I wasn't really listening. I was too busy dragging and dropping, clicking and rotating, moving and stopping, to notice much of anything else that was going on around me.

Until I heard the breathing, of course.

It was a whistle-y kind of nose breathing, heavy and slow, like when you feed cows carrots through a fence and they stick their snouts out at you. And it was sort of menacing. Like if you were facing it, your eyelashes would blow back against your face and your cheeks would smile on their own. And it would smell like onions and danger.

I didn't have to look to know that the breathing was Lunchbox Jones.

My fingers froze on the mouse. I couldn't get them to move. Why was it my body parts refused to cooperate whenever I was around that kid?

"Hey, Lunchbox, what's up? You want to give it a go? Here you are, buddy! Best of luck, old chap," I said, getting up and offering him the computer chair. Oh, wait. No, that was what I *would* have said had my legs not gone numb and slightly warm, making me relatively sure I might have actually peed myself or maybe died. No, no, what I actually said was nothing whatsoever. I just pretended I had no idea a titan was looking over my shoulder and breathing his titan breath onto my skinny little neck.

Mr. Terry came back just as I was getting the feeling back in my fingers.

"How are we doing?" he asked. Clearly he wasn't looking around, or he would have seen that we weren't really doing much of anything at all related to robotics. Though one of the Jacobs had managed to nail the other Jacob's shirt to a workbench, which was somewhat impressive. "Got some programming done, Luke?" He came up behind me and put his hand on my shoulder. I no longer felt the livestock breath on me. "Yes, yes, looks impressive," Mr. Terry said.

I beamed. "Really?"

"Sure, why not. Should we give it a try?"

"On the robot?" I asked.

"Yes, of course on the robot." He picked up the robot and, before I could do anything to argue, hooked it to the computer and downloaded my program. "Maybe we should get Principal McMillan down here to see this," he said.

"Maybe we should try it out first," I suggested, but he was already on the classroom phone, calling the principal's office.

He talked for a few seconds, during which time nobody else in the room seemed to notice or care what was going on, and then hung up.

"As luck would have it, he's still in the building," Mr. Terry said. "He'll get to see the inaugural run of his new winning robot." He held the robot in the air above his head. "Come on, I'll show you how to line this up." I followed him to the table, where he placed the robot in a square in the corner. "This is home," he said. "The only time you can touch your robot is when it's in its home. Otherwise, you lose points. Understand?"

"I think so," I said. "But that program . . ."

"Okay, so which task did you program it to perform? The wall knock-down here? The obstacle course crawl over here?"

I'd had no idea I was supposed to be programming it to perform specific tasks. I'd thought I was just programming it to do . . . stuff. "The, um . . . the thing with the, um . . . the helicopter pad," I bluffed.

Mr. Terry frowned at the map. "I don't see a helicopter pad," he said. Why had I been so specific? I should have gone with "square." Everything on the board looked like a square. "Oh, you must mean this part over here, with the multicolored cross? I can see how that might look like a helicopter pad. Okay." He cleared his throat, then said in a loud voice, "The skipping rope obstacle under way! Prepare for amazement!"

He leaned over the bot and pressed a few buttons on top. It didn't do anything. He glanced up at me. "Ready?"

"Probably not," I said.

"Here we go." He pressed another button on top and the robot whirred into life. Its mandible (that's what I'd started thinking of the grippers as) opened and closed, twice, and its back tires inched forward and back within the home square, as if it were readying itself to take off.

Principal McMillan walked in just as it got going, and to my amazement, it actually did get going. Everyone stopped what they were doing and watched as the robot inched its way out of the home square and onto the board. It went straight to the center of the board and then stopped.

The entire team let out a groan. Even Jacob, who was still wrestling to get his shirt unstuck from the workbench.

"Is that all?" Principal McMillan asked, looking puzzled. "I expected it to have a little more . . . movement."

"I don't know what I—" I started, but Mr. Terry, bent so far over the table his forehead was nearly on top of it, waved his hand to shush me.

"Give it a second, give it a second."

I was still skeptical, but I gave it a second. And, sure enough, the robot started to move again. It looped then stopped, looped then stopped, looped then stopped. It shuddered on its back tires.

"There it goes, there it goes," Mr. Terry said, leaning even closer. "Any minute now it's going to—"

As if the robot could read his mind, it suddenly shot forward at lightning speed right at Mr. Terry's forehead, the tire treads taking a swatch of Mr. Terry's eyebrow with it.

"Yikes!" Mr. Terry yelled, falling backward into the desk behind him.

The robot kept going, launching right over the edge of the table and slamming into Principal McMillan's belt buckle.

"Oof!" Principal McMillan doubled over and fell sideways on the floor.

The robot bounced onto the floor, righted itself, drove over Principal McMillan's chest, shearing off the edge of his necktie, and then took aim at Mikayla. She shrieked and ran out of the room. The robot took off again, anyway, zipping between the Jacobs, ripping the stuck shirt and knocking them both onto their backsides. It zoomed past Stuart, a sprinkling of old sunflower seeds falling out of its motor, which Stuart promptly picked up and stuffed into his mouth.

It zinged around the room a few more times, knocking over the sixth graders' bookshelf projects, crashing into a stack of Plexiglas, and setting off the sanders. I watched it, wincing and flinching every so often, from behind the safety of the computer table. Somehow I'd managed to program it to destroy the entire room except where I was standing. Which, admittedly, was going to look a little fishy.

Finally, the robot raced over to where Lunchbox Jones was standing. Lunchbox stopped it with his foot. He reached down and picked it up, its wheels revving and spinning until he pushed a few buttons to turn it off.

He set the robot back onto the table and walked out of the room.

Slowly, the Jacobs, Mr. Terry, and Principal McMillan pulled themselves off the floor, and Mikayla crept back into the room like a scared deer.

"This is the success you've spent your budget on?" Principal McMillan said. The point of his tie fell off and landed in the skipping-rope square.

Mr. Terry shrugged, looking very quizzical with the piece of his eyebrow missing. "We have some kinks to work out."

"I should say so," Principal McMillan said. A rhinestone was stuck to his cheek. He straightened what was left of his tie, rearranged his belt buckle, and limped out of the room.

Mr. Terry rubbed his bald eyebrow space for a long time

after the principal had gone. He walked over to the table and picked up the robot. He was careful about it, as if he were handling a dangerous animal. "I suppose we should go ahead and call it a day," he said. "Let's meet again on Wednesday. We probably have some catching up to do. Grab a flier on your way out. It's all about the tournament."

I felt like I should say something. *I'm sorry*, maybe. Or *Don't worry, Mr. Terry, it will come out all right.* Or even, *Hey, eyebrows grow back!* But in the moment it seemed like the best thing to do would be to just leave him alone.

We all silently grabbed our backpacks and jackets and fliers and headed for the door.

Mikayla and I got to the door at the same time.

She shook her head at me pathetically.

"I told you it was a large," she said.

# CHAPTER 14

PROGRAM NAME: Disappointment
STEP ONE: Robot zaps alien robots
STEP TWO: Alien robots slip away from
   robot's zapper
STEP THREE: Robot slumps under
   tournament table and pouts

So now I was down to only Tuesdays and Thursdays for playing *Alien Onslaught* with Randy. After the huge disaster that was my attempt at programming, I begged Dad to let me drop out of the team.

"Nope," he said. "You committed and they need you." Dad was always all about "living up to commitments" and "fulfilling your obligations" and all kinds of annoying stuff that was supposed to be about making me a better person.

"I had to make Walter build it, and my program almost killed the principal," I argued. "Plus, nobody ever said anything about Wednesdays. I need my Wednesdays, Dad!"

But Dad was adamant; I was staying on the team.

On Tuesday, when I finally got to log on, Randy was already at level 32, which meant I'd missed the four-eyed alien and the part where you get to rescue baby aliens and put them back in their nests. Both things I had been really looking forward to.

"You should have seen the alien babies," Randy said. "They were really cute. They had these giant lips on their foreheads and their antenna stalks were on their tails. I got to change one's diaper."

"That sounds epic," I said. But I was glum about it.

"Sorry you missed it, man. After we beat the game, we can go back and do it again."

"Sure," I said. "That's cool. No big deal." But it was. It was totally a big deal. Every gamer knew it stunk to play a level for the first time alongside someone who'd already beaten that level before. It wouldn't ever be the same.

We played for a while, and Randy kept trying to cheer me up by making crude noises into the headset every time he captured an alien.

"Did you hear it? I scared the poo right out of him," he said each and every time, and followed it with peals of laughter that made one of my eyes close involuntarily.

I chuckled along as best I could, because I hated for a guy to feel like his best efforts at disgusting hilarity were wasted, but I wasn't feeling it, which only made me madder. It was one of my only two days to play with Randy, and I couldn't get into it.

But then, just as we reached level 35, Dad called me in to clean my stuff off the kitchen table and get ready for dinner.

"Okay, man, see ya," Randy said and then sucked in a gasp of air. "Dude, I almost forgot to tell you!"

"Luke? Did you hear me?" Dad called from the kitchen.

"I gotta go, Randy."

"No, you're going to want to hear this first, I promise you," he said.

"Luke?"

"Just a second, Dad!" I called. "What is it?" I asked into the headset. "Hurry."

"You won't believe it," Randy said. "There's going to be an *Alien Onslaught* tournament. A real, live gamers tournament. In person and everything."

"Really?" I jumped up.

"Yeah. Look it up online. It's in some events center and they're going to have big screens set up and you can register and win all kinds of prizes. It looks completely awesome. And you want to know the best part?"

"Luke? Right! Now!" Dad was getting mad.

"One more second, Dad!" I called. This was too important to worry about getting in trouble now. Randy was just getting to the best part. "What?" I asked Randy.

"It's in Kansas City, and my mom said she'd take me. I'm coming to your city, man. We could register together in the team event."

"No way!" I yelled. I imagined Randy's eye closing

involuntarily at the sound of my voice. But I couldn't help it. He was right—this was big.

"Do you think you can come?" he asked. "My mom said she'd talk to your mom and everything."

"Yes, I am so there. I'll get them to agree to it, whatever it takes. When is it?"

"Luke, I'm not going to ask you again! If you want to play your video game on Thursday, you need to get off it right now."

"It's November twelfth. That's a Saturday," Randy said. "We'll talk about it on Thursday, okay?"

"Definitely," I said. "We are going to win so many prizes."

I disconnected and hurriedly put away my Ultimate Gaming Zone. All I could think about was playing *Alien Onslaught* with Randy in person. We would beat the whole game. We would win the grand prize. Maybe the grand prize was a free copy of *Alien Onslaught 2*. Or maybe we'd get to meet the game's creators. Or maybe we'd win a real, live alien.

*And to our winners-ers-ers goes the grand prize-ize-ize. A four-eyed alien-en-en named Chuck-uck-uck! Luke Abbott and Randy Whateveryournameis, please come claim your prize-ize-ize and be sure to send us all postcards-ards-ards when you visit Chuck's home planet-anet-anet.*

The joy! The epicness! The amazingness!

"The table is not going to clean itself," Dad intoned from the kitchen.

I rushed into the kitchen, my cheeks already hurting from smiling. I gathered my school things together.

"Hey, Dad, guess what? There's an *Alien Onslaught* tournament on November twelfth and Randy is going to be there and his mom said she'd talk to you well actually she said she'd talk to Mom but probably it will be you like usual and we can win stuff and maybe I can even win a real live alien because why not and it's in Kansas City and nothing ever comes to Kansas City and we would totally be the best team there I just know it and can I go?"

"Whoa, sport, let's just worry about dinner right now, okay? It's getting cold."

"But this is really important," I said.

"And we'll talk about it over dinner. Just go put your things away. Mom will be home any minute and we'll eat. And then we'll talk about your alien sports thing."

I rolled my eyes. "It's not a sport. It's a game," I mumbled.

But he was willing to talk about it, so I didn't want to push my luck too much. I took my things to my room. I tossed my jacket onto my bed and set my backpack in my desk chair.

And that's when I saw it.

The robotics flier that I'd laid there yesterday.

The one all about the robotics tournament. The mandatory robotics tournament that the whole team had to go to.

The one that was going to be held on November 12.

# CHAPTER 15

PROGRAM NAME: The Comfort Zone
STEP ONE: Robot is down in the dumps
STEP TWO: Robot Mommy comes to
    rescue
STEP THREE: Robot drowns its cogs in ice
    cream

I'd never been the biggest fan of peas, but that night at dinner I must have pushed them around on my plate even more than usual, because Dad kept asking if I felt okay, and Mom kept putting her hand on my forehead. And every time I told them I was fine, they did that Eyeball Morse Code thing that parents do, where they make certain stare-and-eyebrow-movements at each other, having whole conversations that nobody hears out loud.

They didn't appreciate *Alien Onslaught*, so they couldn't possibly understand why the November 12 robotics tournament would be such a big deal, so why even bother trying to make them understand?

Even worse, halfway through dinner, Rob showed up, completely destroying what would have been left of my appetite.

"Sorry I'm late," he said, scooting into his chair, directly across from mine. "Some of the guys decided to stay after to work out in the weight room."

"Good idea," Dad said, scooping peas into his mouth. "Getting into shape before you go."

Mom made an encouraging noise, but when I looked at her I noticed that her smile was spread thin across her face, like a pencil line, and she didn't seem too thrilled about having to swallow her mouthful of peas. Not that I could blame her. I didn't want to swallow mine, either.

"Some of the guys were saying I should go ahead and shave my head now," Rob went on, forking food into his mouth like this conversation was nothing. Like he didn't notice that he was sitting right across from me, even though I had made it perfectly clear that I didn't want to sit in the same room with him again, ever.

"Shave it already?" Mom practically barked, but then she wiped her mouth with the corner of a napkin and smiled. "How come?" she asked, much more gently.

Rob ran his hand through his hair. I hoped he'd get food stuck in it. Really sticky, smelly food that would rot into a pile of gray slime, and then everyone would call him Slimy. Maybe, just maybe, I could hate the idea of him going off to boot camp a tiny bit less if I knew he was having to answer to the name Private Slimy a hundred times a day. "Just to get used to it, I guess," he said.

"But winter's coming," Mom said. "Won't your—I don't know, your scalp—get cold?"

"Not if I wear hats," Rob said.

"Exactly. You'll wear hats," Dad agreed. "Hats are made for cold scalps."

Though it was a weird thing to say, nobody could exactly argue with his point.

Dad looked up at Mom, grinning and chewing, thrilled to have solved the problem. Mom grinned back, but then she laid her fork across her plate and didn't eat anything else.

Dad and Rob kept talking about hats and haircuts and military bases and stuff, but I mostly tuned them out. Sometimes Dad seemed more excited about Rob going than Rob did. Sometimes I wondered if Dad wished he were going into the marines, too. Mostly, I couldn't understand why these kinds of conversations didn't make him feel nauseous and jittery. Maybe there was something wrong with me. Maybe this was a really exciting thing, and I was crazy for being mad.

They'd finished eating and were carrying their plates to the sink, still talking, when Mom reached over and put her hand on top of mine.

"Want to go get ice cream for dessert?" she asked. "Just me and you?"

I didn't feel like dessert, but I wasn't the kind of guy who would ever turn down ice cream. Plus, going to get ice cream meant getting away from Rob, so I was all in.

At first, Mom was really quiet, her mouth staying in that pencil line shape most of the way to the ice cream shop. I was enjoying the silence. I was maybe even beginning to think I was in the mood for ice cream after all, and had begun assembling my sundae in my head. Contrary to popular belief, ice cream sundaes were not something one simply goes and buys. Sundae assembly was a science.

## The Luke Abbott Method
## to Perfect Sundae Assembly:

- **Layer one:** Chocolate sauce, the thin kind that sort of tastes like a can.
- **Layer two:** Vanilla ice cream. Not ice milk. Never ice milk. What kind of dessert-hating monster invented ice milk, anyway?
- **Layer three:** Mini marshmallows, or any sort of gummy candy that tricks your brain into forgetting you were eating ice cream, until . . .
- **Layer four:** More vanilla ice cream. A really thick layer.
- **Layer five:** Exactly two squirts of warm peanut butter sauce. None must touch the side. If a drop of peanut butter sauce touches the side of the cup, you must throw it all away and start over.
- **Layer six:** A swooshy layer of chocolate ice cream that tests the very laws of gravity, leaning over to one side so far, old ladies make gasping noises and whip out napkins every time you move.

🍨 **Layer seven:** Hot fudge. Thick, gooey hot fudge that completely covers all the ice cream. Someone looking at the top of your sundae must think that you are holding a cup of hot fudge only. Which would not be an entirely bad idea, actually.

🍨 **Layer eight:** A drizzle of caramel, using a zigzag method. Exactly three zigs; exactly four zags. There may be no clumps of caramel. If you will have to chew, you must throw it away and start all over again. This is science, people! It must be exact!

🍨 **Layer nine:** A cherry, even though cherries are really gross, but your mom likes them so you order one just to give it to her. It's your way of saying thank you for all the times she saved your cheeks from the maws.

But just as we pulled into the ice cream shop parking lot and parked the car, instead of getting out, Mom took a deep breath and looked at me very seriously.

"I know you hate it that your brother's leaving," she said. Aha. The real reason she wanted to get ice cream.

I groaned, flopping my head back against the seat rest. I should have seen the ice cream trick coming. Moms were crafty. They almost never suggested unhealthy food without a catch.

"It's okay, Luke," she said. "I hate it, too."

I opened one eye and turned my head to look at her,

surprised. "Really? I thought everybody thought it was the best idea ever. The aws do. Dad does. I figured I was the only one."

"Well, it is the best idea for Rob," she said. "But it makes me scared. I think it probably makes you scared, too, huh?"

I tried to shake my head. I was mad, not scared. Only babies and girls got scared. Manly men got mad. And I was a manly man, so I was . . . okay, I was scared. And I could never hide anything from my mom. I nodded. "Sort of," I said. "But I'm mostly just scared that he'll forget about me."

Mom nodded, like she totally got it, and shifted back in her seat, too. "You know, when he was two years old he asked for an army set for Christmas. I didn't even know what an army set was. And I was shocked that he did." She ran her thumbnail around the steering wheel, knocking dirt out of crevices while she talked. But her eyes looked like they were looking at something much farther away than the steering wheel. "So we found him an olive green shirt, some camouflage pants, a canteen, little boots, a compass, binoculars. He was so happy. He didn't care about anything else he got that year. We thought we'd never get him out of those clothes. Dad would wash them, and Rob would put them right back on the next day. Sometimes he refused to take them off at bedtime.

"Of course, that was before you were born," she said, glancing over at me. "And we thought it would just be a phase. But after you came along, he had someone to play army with. And he never seemed to get over it. You loved playing it, too, right?"

"Yeah, I guess." Of course I loved playing it. That was the problem. I loved playing it, and I would still love playing it, but now it was real for Rob, and I could make all the walkie-talkie noises with my mouth in the world, but it wouldn't be good enough. Not compared to the real thing.

She reached over and put her hand on my arm. "So I keep telling myself, this is what Rob has been wanting to do since he was two years old. And that makes it the best thing for him. And it scares me to death, thinking about him being sent to a strange, dangerous place. But I have to let him go because I love him. And you and I will just have to eat a lot of ice cream while he's gone."

"You mean eat a lot of ice cream forever, because he won't come back."

"He won't forget you, Luke," she said. "He'll be back."

"Yeah, but it won't be the same," I said.

"Nope, probably not exactly the same," Mom said. She pulled her keys out of the ignition and dropped them into her purse. "But he'll still be your brother."

"He's not my brother. My brother wouldn't just go off and leave like this," I said, surprising myself. I hadn't spoken to Rob in a long time, so my parents knew I was mad at him, but I hadn't really said out loud what I was thinking.

"Oh, Luke," Mom said, pressing her hand to my cheek. Even though I was mad and trying to be tough, I couldn't help but lean into her cool palm. I don't care how mad or tough a guy is, a mom hand is a mom hand, period. "It's eating Rob up inside that you're so mad at him. And I know it's eating you up, too. Why don't you try to forgive him? It would mean a lot to me."

*No*, I wanted to scream. *I'll never forgive the traitor!* I wanted to rant and rave and make her, and everyone else, understand why I was so upset about him leaving. But I met Mom's gaze and it looked so hopeful, and her palm felt so cool on my cheek, I couldn't do it. "I'll try," I said, even though on the inside I knew I wouldn't.

Mom smiled, and this time her lips weren't stretched-out worms, but actual smile-lips. "Good," she said. "I was hoping you'd say that." She unbuckled her seat belt and slid her purse strap up onto her shoulder. "Now. Are you ready to build one of your famous nine-layer sundaes?"

I tried my best to smile. "Sure," I said.

But I must not have been very convincing, because she paused with her hand clutching the door handle and frowned at me. "Is there something else bothering you, Luke? You haven't been yourself lately."

Immediately I thought about November 12th, when Randy would be battling aliens without me, and when I'd be battling Missy the Cruel on my own team. My stomach twisted up into half-angry, half-sad knots, and suddenly there I was again, not hungry. And on nine-layer sundae day, too. The cruelty of robotics would never end.

But Mom already seemed so bothered by the thing with Rob. Worried about him, worried about me, probably worried that we would never speak again, or that Rob would go off to a war thinking I hated him. And who knew what other sad things moms thought about. I didn't want to add to it.

"Nope, I'm good," I said, forcing a big nine-layer-sundae-eating smile.

It must have been convincing, because Mom's frown disappeared and she pushed open her door.

"Dibs on the cherry," she called as we headed up the walk to the ice cream shop door.

# CHAPTER 16

PROGRAM NAME: Enemy Down
STEP ONE: Rabid robot returns to mat
STEP TWO: Rabid robot moves to new
  home base
STEP THREE: All other robots cheer and
  toss their pincers in the air

I couldn't have been any less motivated to go to robotics on Wednesday. Now it wasn't just messing with my gaming on Monday and Wednesday. It was messing with the greatest gaming tournament of all time. It was messing with my life, and I didn't like it one bit.

The only thing that could have made practice worse was for Missy to be back.

So of course she was. She was standing by the computer with her hands on her hips when I walked into the room.

"I heard you messed up the robot," she said. "Way to go, Loser Luke. I'm not surprised, by the way. You mess up everything."

"Even wishes," I said. "Because I was wishing you wouldn't come back and here you are."

Missy looked shocked. I'd never outright fought back with her before. I pulled up one side of my lip and tried for a menacing snaggletooth grimace just to drive the point home. Apparently I was in no mood to be messed with today.

"Well, you may be better at wishes than you know," she said, and I couldn't tell if that was supposed to be an insult—like *You're so bad at messing things up, you even mess up messing up*—or if I detected a tiny hint of sadness in her voice. "And what's wrong with your lip?" she added.

But before I could say anything, the rest of the team arrived, Stuart's pockets bulging so far out he almost had to turn sideways to get through the door. He was definitely not going to run out of seeds again.

Mr. Terry came in right after them, a bandage placed over his eyebrow. I'd heard him tell a kid in Life Skills class that he'd cut it while boxing at the gym. I couldn't blame him. What guy would want to tell other guys that his face got beat up by a three-pound plastic toy?

"Okay, troops, we have a lot of ground to cover," he said. He slapped a giant manual down on the robotics table. "So let's get started. First off, we need to learn how the programming works, so we can minimize future, er . . . accidents."

"Is Principal McMillan okay?" a Jacob asked.

"I heard he's in the hospital," the other Jacob added. "I heard it's bad. Really bad."

"Oh, we should put together a fund-raiser," Mikayla said.

"I'll take charge of the talent portion. I know just which talent to feature." She kicked off one flip-flop and fanned her toes.

Mr. Terry held out his hands. "No need to put together anything. Principal McMillan is totally fine. He's in his office, not at the hospital. He and both of his eyebrows." He touched the bandage gingerly. "Now, we really need to focus on the tasks at hand. This robot will be competing against other robots in less than a month, and he isn't even programmed to get out of the start box."

"Um, excuse me, Mr. Terry?" Missy asked, raising her hand, doing her Inquisitive Student Act that everyone who ever had a class with her knew oh so well. It was one of her more annoying classroom traits, of which I had compiled a comprehensive list.

**Missy Farnham's Most Annoying Classroom Traits:**

1. The Inquisitive Student Act, where she raises her hand and her eyebrows and asks the teacher a question that she already knows the answer to but also knows is just the kind of question that will impress the teacher and make him say he wishes more students were like her.

2. The Extra Credit Act, where she tells the teacher that she "accidentally" finished all the work way ahead of everyone else and is wondering if there's any way she can go above and beyond.

3. The Rat Out a Quiz Act, where she gently reminds a teacher who has forgotten that we have a quiz that she knows nobody else in the class has studied for.
4. The Missy the Cruel Act, where she acts like herself.

"Yes, Missy?" Mr. Terry looked a little pained. Maybe he was on to her annoying classroom traits, too. This was a possibility that rocked my world a little. What if even the teachers didn't like Missy Farnham? That almost seemed kind of sad.

"I was just wondering . . . how do you know our robot is a boy?"

"I'm sorry?"

"You said *he* isn't programmed to get out of the start box, but I wasn't sure how you knew he was a boy."

"You know, that's a pretty good point," Mikayla added. "He does have a lot of jewels on him. I think he looks much more girlish than boyish."

"I built him," Missy snapped at Mikayla, and then gathered her face into a sweet smile for Mr. Terry. "I mean, when I was designing her, I was clearly picturing a girl. In fact, I'd kind of named her Rosie."

"Rosie?" the Jacobs said in unison. They also wrinkled their noses in unison. If there were such a sport as Synchronized Jacob-ing, these guys would have a million trophies.

Missy narrowed her eyes at them. "Yes. Rosie the Rallying Robo-Raccoon."

"Aw, that's pretty," Mikayla said. "I agree, she looks like a Rosie."

Mr. Terry was rubbing his eyelids. "Okay," he said steadily. "She's a girl. Fine. It doesn't really matter. Rosie doesn't know how to get out of the start box, either. So let's start with page one." He opened the giant manual.

"She would have if I'd been here," Missy muttered.

Mr. Terry stopped. "Do you know how to program, Missy?"

"Of course I do," she said.

Oh, yeah, I forgot:

5. The Know-It-All Act, where she suddenly knows even more than the teacher and isn't afraid to show it.

"Wonderful!" Mr. Terry exclaimed. "We have our programmer, you guys." He slammed the book shut, picked up the robot, and presented it to Missy. But she kept her arms crossed and didn't take it.

"No, you don't," she said.

"What do you mean?" Mr. Terry asked.

"I mean, I can't program for you."

"Why not? I thought you said you could do it," I said, waiting for the delicious moment when Missy was going to have to admit that she was only bluffing and didn't know how to program the robot at all. "That wasn't a lie, was it?" I pressed, leaning in eagerly.

"Of course it wasn't a lie, glue-eater," she spat. "It's not that hard to program a dumb robot, you know."

I tried not to let that one sting, given that programming our robot had seemed pretty much impossible to me.

She turned back to Mr. Terry and sighed. "I was going to wait and tell you privately," she said. "But since you're all so rudely staring at me, I guess I'll say it now. I was gone last week because I was at my grandma's. My dad moved out and my mom and brother and I have to go live with my grandma now. So I'm changing schools. Starting next week, I'm going to be at Goat Grove." She swiveled toward me. "Are you satisfied?"

Actually, I wasn't. Even though I really, really wanted to be. Missy the Cruel, moving away at last! I had wished and prayed for this day for most of my life. And now it was happening. And I wasn't satisfied. I was a little sad for her.

I tried to imagine what it would be like if Dad moved out on me and Mom and Rob. I tried to picture living with Maw Shirley and Paw Morris and having Friday dinners without him and watching bowling tournaments without him and riding the school bus home from school without Dad asking me questions in a robot voice. I couldn't even envision it. It would be terrible.

I must not have been the only one to think so. Mikayla made a little squeaky noise and flung her arms around Missy's shoulders. The Jacobs shuffled their feet and cleared their throats a bunch.

Stuart stopped chewing and said, "Wow, Missy, that stinks."

"I feel so sorry for you," Mikayla wailed into Missy's shirt.

At first Missy looked startled, and then her face hardened into something else. She shrugged out of Mikayla's hug disgustedly. "Stop it. This is why I was going to tell Mr. Terry in private. I don't need people feeling sorry for me just because my dumb dad moved out. And I especially don't need losers like you guys feeling sorry for me. I don't even care that he moved out. I won't miss him at all. I don't care if I never lay my eyes on him again. As far as I'm concerned, he might as well be dead."

We all stood around in stunned silence. Even Missy looked like she couldn't believe someone had just said that. Her eyes were round and her mouth was hanging open.

And then suddenly there was a noise in the back of the room. Something between a cough and a growl. We turned just in time to see Lunchbox Jones pick up his backpack and his lunchbox and storm out of the room, knocking into two desks on his way out. After he left, we heard the metal clang of something—a fist, maybe?—hitting a locker. We all jumped, even Mr. Terry, and then went back to awkwardly standing around, nobody sure what was supposed to happen next.

Finally Missy seemed to snap out of it. She picked up her bag and slung it over her shoulder. "Well, it's true," she said and flounced out of the room, her ponytail bouncing up and down between her tiny shoulder blades between every step.

Mr. Terry shuffled back to the table and set the robot down, then picked up the manual again. "I guess that means we're back to square one," he said, opening the book on the computer table. "Let's start with what makes a robot a robot. According to this book, a robot is a machine that is able to perform actions that are controlled by a computer." He patted the computer monitor as if he were petting a dog's head. "The robot can be designed to look like an animal or a human, and—"

"Mr. Terry?" one of the Jacobs asked.

Mr. Terry stopped, looking almost afraid of what might come from this interruption. "Yes, Jacob?"

"Does this mean we have to keep the name Rosie?"

# CHAPTER 17

PROGRAM NAME: The Strong, Silent Bot
STEP ONE: Bot runs into other bot
STEP TWO: Bot talks to other bot
STEP THREE: Other bot's system crashes
 and stalls out

By Thursday morning, it had really sunk in that Missy was leaving Forest Shade Middle School. Now that I wasn't listening to her sad and awkward story about her dad leaving, I could pretend that it was nothing but good news. No more Loser Luke, no more glue-eater songs, no more spending time daydreaming that a monkey would escape from the zoo, come to Forest Shade, burst into Missy's first period class, and fling poo into her hair. I could spend my daydreaming time on something much more productive. Like how I was going to get to that *Alien Onslaught* tournament.

My current plan involved somehow exposing all the

Forest Shade Robo-Raccoons except myself to smallpox so they would have to be quarantined. It was a long shot, but it was all I had.

"Walter, my man!" I shouted while I was still half a hallway away from my locker. His spine straightened, unsure. "What's on tap today? Pop Rocks? Chocolate-covered mints? Homemade caramels? You know how I love your mom's homemade caramels. Hit me with it!" I had reached him with my palm outstretched. At first he just gazed at my hand uncertainly, but then he dug into the front pocket of his backpack and pulled out a pink-and-white-striped straw.

"Pixy Stix!" he said. I took the straw.

"Excellent. Today is a Pixy Stix kind of day."

"Oh, and . . ." He rummaged around in his coat pocket and pulled out a limp licorice whip. "I saved yours from the other day. I figured you'd want it when you felt better."

I gave the licorice a dubious look. It had Walter's coat lint stuck to it, and maybe some dog fur, too, which was weird because Walter didn't own a dog. But mostly it looked okay, and it was a licorice whip kind of day, too. Heck, with Missy the Cruel leaving, it was an All the Candy in the World kind of day. I took the whip, blew off the big chunks, and stuffed the rest into my mouth.

I opened my locker and, as always, the now-empty ripped box sprang out. I kicked it back inside, parked my backpack, and headed toward gym.

"So what's got you in such a good mood?" Walter asked. "I haven't seen you like this since you beat the Neptunian overlord in level nine."

"That was level ten," I said. "And Missy Farnham is moving. They're finally beaming her back to her home planet."

"I don't know her," Walter said. "Is she a seventh grader?"

"Yep." I ripped off the top of the Pixy Stix tube, tipped back my head, and dumped the whole thing into my mouth at once. I'd never mentioned Missy to Walter before. Since he was in sixth grade, I figured they had no classes together, and I kind of liked having one kid in my life who didn't know about the puke song.

"Ex-girlfriend?" He wiggled his eyebrows up and down.

"You bite your tongue," I said around the sugar in my mouth. "The only mammal who would date her belongs in a cage." I felt a tiny stab of guilt over talking about Missy like that, given the rough time she was going through. But then I remembered about a million jumped ropes with my puke-eating name all over them, and I instantly didn't feel so bad anymore. "Let's just say she and I were not best friends, and I might throw her a good-bye party. Everyone but Missy is invited."

"Wow," Walter said. "You mean I get to go to a seventh-grader party? I've never been to one before. What are they like? Do they have balloons? Do people kiss in the closets? Does anyone bring pickles? I like pickles. I should bring pickles. Is everybody really tall? What should I wear? Are Hawaiian shirts acceptable?"

We had reached the point where Walter and I usually parted ways for first period. I stopped and put my hand on his shoulder. "Dude. I'm not really going to have a party.

But if I did, you would be the only sixth grader I'd invite. I promise."

Walter's face lit up. "Really? Thanks, Luke. I think your imaginary party will be the best party I've ever been invited to."

I squeezed his shoulder a couple of times. "That's sad. But you're welcome."

Walter went on his way, and I started to head into the gym, but at the last minute, my eye roved toward the corner by the guidance office, where I'd gone into the restroom a few days before. I wondered if Lunchbox Jones was in there now. It was weird how he'd left the robotics meeting yesterday, and part of me was curious what was really going on with that kid. But the other part of me—the part that hated being punched—didn't care at all why Lunchbox did the things that he did. That part of me just wanted to be able to walk to gym class on legs that weren't twisted into pretzels in a bathroom behind the guidance office.

But, still . . .

The warning bell rang and kids started streaming around me into the gym. If I was going to make a quick restroom stop, this was my opportunity. Coach Verde didn't like tardies. If you were tardy, he made you run an extra lap in warm-up.

I mashed my lips together, feeling the stickiness of left-over Pixy Stix dust on them.

I could hardly go to PE with Pixy Stix dust stuck to me. With my luck, a bee would fly out of a three-leafed clover on the football field and sting me on the lips.

That was all the reason I needed.

I headed toward the bathroom, my legs growing cold with every step closer to Lunchbox Jones. But I kept telling myself that today was Missy Is Leaving Day, and it was such a good day, it was sure to be filled with nothing but good luck. Not only would I find Lunchbox in the bathroom, I told myself, but we would become friends. We would high-five over the great news and would share a paper towel to celebrate. No, actually sharing a paper towel is gross, but you get the point.

"Isn't it a glorious day? Sun is in the sky, birds are in the trees, and Missy Farnham is going to Goat Grove!" I cried as I put both palms on the wooden door.

I burst into the bathroom with more force than I even knew I had. In fact, I burst through the door with so much force, had someone been standing on the other side of it, the door might have hit them right in the face and knocked them backward onto the mildewed floor with the ripped pieces of toilet paper and the upside-down dead beetle by the radiator. I might have even burst through the door so hard that if a person were standing on the other side of it and had been hit in the face and knocked backward onto the floor with the mildew and the toilet paper and the dead beetle, they might get a bloody nose from the impact. And if I had burst through the door with so much force that a person standing on the other side, bloody, had fallen to the mildew and the bugs and toilet paper, they might drop their lunchbox on the way down.

And it might, on its way down, hit the side of the first stall with a *thunk*.

And the lid of said lunchbox might pop open, a hunk of the plastic handle skittering across the tile and coming to a stop with the dead beetle and the scraps of toilet paper and the blood.

And the lid of said now-broken lunchbox might then flop closed again, off-kilter.

My mouth was still formed on the "v" of "Grove." My hand was still on the door. My other hand, betrayer, was flung up in the air in a victory pose that I hadn't even been aware of striking.

I stared at Lunchbox. He stared at me, his hand over his leaking nose.

"Um," I said. "I didn't . . ."

His brow furrowed. His eyes turned into bright red lasers, and his free hand creaked into a leathery fist.

So I did what any upstanding guy who'd just accidentally mowed down Lunchbox Jones would have done.

I ran for my life.

# CHAPTER 18

PROGRAM NAME: Sitting Duck
STEP ONE: Robot zooms to corner of table
STEP TWO: Robot trembles in corner of table making pathetic terrified beep noises
STEP THREE: Robot shorts out with puff of smoke

If you were ever looking for a way to make the football unit more miserable, you should consider accidentally beating up the scariest guy in school right before class.

I spent most of the period looking over my shoulder, praying that Lunchbox wouldn't appear, tie me to the girls' locker room door, and throw dodgeballs at my head. I didn't even mind running the extra tardy lap (I would have made it on time, but I kind of had to make a little detour to a different bathroom to throw up), because at least then I was already moving. One thing about being a little guy trying to avoid a giant like Lunchbox—I could probably outrun him if I had to. The question was for how long.

Once we got outside, the terror only became worse. There wasn't one door to watch; there was the entire outdoors. At one point a grasshopper landed on my leg and I ran in panicked circles for a solid two minutes.

I was so busy being frightened, I hardly even noticed that the rest of the class had somehow managed to get through an entire football game without sending one guy to the nurse's office. I even looked for Brian Blye to make sure he wasn't stuck in a tree or facedown on the parking lot or something.

I found him, in the end zone, squatting in a ready position, hands on his knees, looking like he might have actually known what he was doing a little bit.

"Hey, what's the deal?" I asked Roger Sherman, who was sitting in the grass next to me playing some dinosaur game on his cell phone.

"What?" he said. "I'm bored."

"No, I mean what's the deal with Brian?" I pointed toward the end zone. "When did he start . . . not getting injured?"

Roger shrugged. "Coach talked a bunch of guys into joining the team. They've been practicing for a few weeks now. I guess he's just getting better at it."

I scanned the field. I hadn't noticed, but sure enough, Roger was right. Several of the boys were squatting just like Brian. One of them hiked a football between his legs. It sailed over the shoulder of the quarterback, but two other guys went for it. And they didn't bump heads to pick it up. They were improving.

"Did everybody join?" I asked.

Roger's thumb worked frantically over his phone screen. "Almost. I think Coach promised to take them to some big video game tournament in November if they signed up."

"What?" I couldn't believe it. If I'd signed up for football, not only would the paws have been happy, I'd have gotten to go to the *Alien Onslaught* tournament. I'd have even been able to claim it was a school function so Mom and Dad would have had no choice but to let me go. "So unfair," I said.

"If you like that sort of thing," Roger said. "I didn't sign up, and now I get to sit out during gym class and play games on my phone, and Coach doesn't even notice. They get to go to one tournament. I get to play for an hour every day without anyone yelling at me. And I won't get a concussion trying to beat Goat Grove. Awesome, right?"

As if to punctuate his point, the guy in the middle of the field snapped again, and the ball got stuck in the quarterback's face mask. Panicked, he ran forward, knocking down six other guys before Coach could catch him and stop him.

"Yeah, I guess you have a point," I said.

The rest of the day went by slowly. Missy was especially annoying in all our classes, like she was trying to set a record of annoyingness so we wouldn't forget her after she left. Walter ran out of Pixy Stix before lunch. I couldn't stop stewing about the fact that Brian Blye, who probably didn't even play *Alien Onslaught*, was going to be at the tournament and I wasn't. And my smallpox plan was starting to look like it might have a few holes in it.

My mood had turned all the way around, and what had begun as the best day ever ended up as the worst day ever. At least it was Thursday, so I'd get to play with Randy for a while.

I was so happy when the final bell rang, I wasn't even paying attention to where I was going until I got to my locker and ran chest-to-chest into Lunchbox Jones.

I gasped, trying not to look him in the face, using the same advice they give you at the zoo not to look directly at the gorillas so you don't incite a riot. But I couldn't help looking. Last I'd seen him, he was cupping his nose, and I wouldn't have been surprised to find his nose all swollen and mangled and maybe even missing from the way it had been bleeding.

It wasn't any of those things. It was maybe a little pink on the end, and I could see some brown dried blood crust around the edge of one nostril, but otherwise it looked totally fine.

It was the two black eyes that didn't look fine at all.

"Excuse me," I squeaked out, suddenly all perfect gentleman-style. I may have even adopted a British accent. "I was just getting to my locker here."

Lunchbox didn't move. He also didn't speak. He seemed to be totally happy to just be standing there making me tremble. The handle of his lunchbox had been taped.

"Um, I'm sorry about your nose," I said. "And your, um, lunchbox. And the toilet paper and stuff."

He continued to stare at me. His nostrils flared a little, like a bull's. It made me think of the breathing he'd done down my back at robotics practice.

"So, um, no hard feelings?" I held out my hand as if to shake, but he only glanced at it and made no move to take it. "You know, I'll just come back to my locker later. Tomorrow or something. I don't really need my jacket. It's not that cold out. I like it when it's a little brisk. Gets the old bones working." Great, now I was a perfect senior citizen gentleman. Soon I'd be calling him "sonny" and shuffling off for my four o'clock bowl of oatmeal.

To my surprise, he moved then. Just a long step to the side, wide enough for me to get to my locker. He watched as I fumbled with the combination, having to try it twice before it would work, kicked the torn box back inside, and grabbed my jacket.

"So I'll see ya," I said, moving away slowly, going off the zoo advice that you should never run from a stalking cheetah.

Once far enough away, I turned and headed toward the door. I could already see Dad's car out there. It was so far away.

Just as I reached the double doors, I heard it.

Low, growly, unmistakable. Hard to believe, but definitely there.

"See ya, Luke," it said.

Only it sounded normal.

(with no car alarms going off or windshields shattering or stuff.)

# CHAPTER 19

PROGRAM NAME: Discovery
STEP ONE: Robot picks up lots of junk
STEP TWO: Robot finds jewels in junk
STEP THREE: Robot stuffs jewels into
cheeks like a squirrel

The next day was a teacher in-service day. Nobody really knew what that meant, only that we got a free day at home. No getting up early, no eating cardboard pizza in the cafeteria for lunch, no having your head popped off by a lunchbox-carrying maniac between first and second periods.

And all *Alien Onslaught* all day.

Randy did have school, so it was my turn, for a change, to beat some levels. I popped a bag of popcorn, poured myself a soda, and settled into the Ultimate Gaming Zone.

But Dad had different plans. He appeared just as I slipped the first bite of popcorn between my teeth.

"Come on, Luke. Put the headset down. We're going to clean out the garage."

"What? No way. Don't make me. I don't want to."

I knew this was no way to get Dad to change his mind. In fact, Dad never changed his mind on anything, ever. So it was a wasted effort, but I had to try. It was sort of my job as a kid.

"You can play when the garage is clean. Come on, the sooner we get out there, the sooner you can do your alien thing."

I groaned, put down the controller, and followed him. "My soda will be flat by the time I get back," I grumbled, but he didn't care.

The first half hour was the worst. We straightened the ball bucket from when Rob and I used to play catch together. I told Dad he might as well throw all of that out, since Rob was definitely not going to be throwing anything to me anymore, but Dad kept it all. We went through Dad's old tools, throwing away bent nails and rusty screwdrivers. We aired the tires on Mom's bicycle and stood the rakes and shovels and hoes up in one corner. They kept falling over and thunking me on the back of the head.

Winter was definitely coming, and it was starting to get cold and gray outside. My fingers were numb, which made it hard to pick up the tiny screws that had fallen over on one shelf, and my nose kept running.

But somewhere after that first half hour it started not being so bad anymore. Dad and I took turns making up stories about horrible things that happened to guys while they were cleaning the garage. He taught me songs that Paw Morris had learned in the navy and had passed down to Dad when he was a little boy. Most of them had bad words and Dad had to keep reminding me not to let Mom ever hear me sing them.

And then Dad talked about what life was like when he was a kid. How he could ride his bike for hours around the neighborhood and nobody would ever ask him where he was going or where he'd been. He talked about how Maw Mazie was the best cook in the neighborhood and everyone would always come over to eat with them.

He told me about the first time he met Mom. They were little kids and she was outside selling lemonade. He thought she was cute, so he paid five whole dollars for a cup. And then she let him sell it with her, and they spit in Clyde Pill's lemonade because Clyde always picked on Dad because Dad was smaller than him. Dad said when he saw that white loogie hanging off Mom's lip and dropping into Clyde's lemonade, he knew right then and there that he would love her forever. He said it took a lot more years, though, for Mom to decide she loved him back.

We worked while we sang and made up stories and talked, and within another hour, we'd almost finished. Dad got the broom and started sweeping dirt and leaves outside, and I rummaged in a back corner. I found a trunk full of old books there, including an old yearbook from Forest Shade Middle School.

"Is this yours?" I asked, pulling out the book and sitting on the bumper of his car to leaf through it.

"Would you look at that," he said. "I haven't seen that old thing in years. Yep, that's mine. But Mom's in there, too, of course. Seventh grade."

I turned to the index in the back and found Dad's name. It listed three pages he was pictured on.

The first was his school picture from that year. I laughed out loud. His hair was sticking straight up in the back, and his thick glasses made his eyes look huge. He had a big, goofy grin on his face, showing all his teeth, covered by what looked like twenty-seven pounds of steel.

"Braces were a lot more of an ordeal when I was your age," he said. "You're lucky you don't have to have them."

"You were really funny looking back then, Dad," I said, though the truth was he was mostly really happy looking. Like he'd never had a Missy the Cruel or a Lunchbox Jones or even a Clyde Pill to worry about, even though I knew he did.

"I was pretty funny looking, wasn't I?" he asked.

I turned to the second page he was listed on. The page was full of photos from a school dance. Dad was front and center, slow dancing with a blond girl, the same spiky hair and same goofy grin on his face. The girl's hands were on Dad's shoulders, and she was smiling shyly at the camera.

"That's not Mom," I said.

"Nope, that was Carla Hall. Quiet little thing. She agreed to go to the dance with me that year because Maw Mazie promised to make us sloppy joes before the dance."

"She went with you for a sloppy joe?"

"I've told you, Maw's cooking was a powerful force in the neighborhood. Don't tell Maw Shirley, but Maw Mazie's corned beef hash was legendary."

"Gross, people liked that back then?" I shuddered and turned to the last page that was listed by Dad's name. "What the . . . ?"

It was the clubs page, and Dad's club was pictured on the top right. And there was Dad, standing front and center in a lab coat and safety goggles, holding a clunky-looking piece of metal proudly toward the camera.

"The Future Club?" I asked.

Dad nodded. "Or what you might have called a future robotics club. We built small machines, battery powered, and raced them. They didn't do all the amazing things your robots can do today, of course. But they could use a few double-A batteries to drive in a straight line, and it was pretty gnarly."

"What is gnarly?"

"Our version of epic."

"Oh, so gnarly meant awesome."

He shook his head. "No, we had awesome. Awesome meant awesome. Really awesome was bogus. Really bogus was tubular. And that robot right there? The one that I built with my own two hands? That robot was fully gnarly."

It didn't really look all that gnarly to me. It looked big and clumsy and square, and like it wouldn't have won a single race.

"Did it win?" I asked.

"Not a single race," Dad said. Yep, just as I thought.

"Oh."

"Well, it wasn't really the robot's fault. You see, the whole team got smallpox and we had to be quarantined for two whole weeks."

I gasped. "Really?"

Dad winked at me. "No, of course not. I heard you telling Randy your plan the other night. I don't suppose you've found a supplier for your live smallpox strain?"

"No, the plan has some complications," I said.

"I see." He leaned the broom against the wall and sat next to me on the bumper. "You know, Luke," he said, "I had the best time building that robot. The entire world was possible, and it was up to me to decide what that world would look like. It was the most powerful time of my entire life, because there were no boundaries. I could make happen whatever I wanted to make happen, just because I believed. We didn't have robots back then, not like you do now. But I could build one, and it could look like this and it could race forward and who knew what else it could do? It was up to me to dream that up. Do you understand what I'm saying?"

"Not really," I said.

"I'm saying," he said, ruffling my hair the way he always did whenever he felt we were having a moment together, "you have the power right now to believe in whatever you want to believe in. You can believe that you can make a robot. You can believe that you will lead your robotics team to victory, and you can believe that you will have fun doing it. And maybe even make a few lifelong friends. Friends who'll hawk loogies into lemonade with you, if that's what's necessary. You can believe anything you want. Pretty cool, huh?"

I nodded, because I was pretty sure he'd just made a really big point that I just wasn't really getting at all yet.

"You can even believe," he said, giving me a Dad look, "that you and your brother will still have a great relationship, even though he's leaving."

Ah. There it was. The point.

"Okay," I said.

"Excellent," he said. He stood up and went back to his broom. "I'll finish up in here. You should get some aliens defeated before the maws and paws get here and steal the TV away from you."

I sat there a moment longer and stared at the picture of Dad holding his robot. He looked so happy, like he totally believed in that bot. I closed the book, but stayed on the bumper holding it on my lap for a while.

"So why didn't you win?" I asked.

He shrugged while still sweeping, his back to me. "Because we're Forest Shade Middle School. We don't win. It's sort of our thing."

# CHAPTER 20

PROGRAM NAME: Pep Talk of Doom
STEP ONE: Robot climbs on podium
STEP TWO: Robot gives amazing speech
STEP THREE: Robot gets hit in head with
rotten tomato and falls off podium

For reasons I couldn't quite understand, I wasn't dreading our Monday robotics meeting as much as usual. Sure, it may have had something to do with Missy being officially gone, but there was also this little matter of Lunchbox Jones, black eyes and all, being there. I was hoping that him not stuffing me into my locker the week before was a good sign that maybe he wasn't quite as mad as I'd expected him to be.

I decided to press my luck that morning with another trip to the restroom before gym. This time, I pushed the door open gently, at first just a few inches, and then, after seeing that he wasn't directly on the other side of it, opening it fully.

Once inside, I wasn't quite sure what to do. I mean, I generally know what to do in a restroom. I'd pretty much known that since I was two. But I didn't really have to do those things at the moment, and standing around trying to do those things right next to Lunchbox Jones seemed like a pretty scary move.

As usual, Lunchbox was at the sink. His jacket was on the radiator, his repaired lunchbox balanced on top of it. His chin was dripping, and so were the edges of his hair, and his face was red as if it had just been scrubbed. He looked at me in the mirror. His eyes had purple smudges beneath them, but they were small smudges, and his nose looked like a normal nose.

He paused, I paused, we both stared, it was uncomfortable. I sort of wished I'd stopped while I was ahead and had just gone to gym without nosing into Lunchbox's business. But I couldn't help myself. I was curious. Why was he in here washing up every morning? All kinds of theories were running through my head. The current favorite was that he was an escapee from juvenile detention and was hiding in the woods at night, eating raw squirrels and painting his face with mud so he could blend in with his surroundings. It was possible—those kinds of things happened in TV shows all the time.

I bent my knees, just in case he should turn into a muscle-bulging super-villain and I should need to bolt, but after a few seconds, Lunchbox went back to his washing, and then turned to the paper towel dispenser and started rolling off a long sheet of paper towel.

Slowly, I walked to the sink next to his and turned on the water. I cupped my hands underneath the faucet, and then bent over the sink and splashed the water on my face. It was cold, and some of it went down the front of my shirt. But I pretended I didn't notice. I gathered another handful and splashed it over my face, too. And then a third.

By then, Lunchbox was done drying his face and had put his jacket back on. The warning bell rang, and he picked up his lunchbox and left the room. I saw all of this in my peripheral vision, of course. To Lunchbox, I was so busy studying my wet face in the mirror, I didn't even notice he was gone.

Alone in the bathroom, I stared at where he'd just been, then ripped off my own paper towels and dried my face. I hadn't needed to wash up—I'd taken a shower that morning—but that wasn't the point.

I had gotten held up cleaning up my art supplies in seventh period, so by the time I got to robotics, the rest of the team was already there. Mr. Terry was fussing with the computer. He seemed to be having troubles getting it to boot up, and everyone except Lunchbox had gathered around to check out the problem.

"There seems to be a program interfering," Mr. Terry said, scratching the top of his head. "It keeps telling me to open it up."

"So open it," I said.

Mr. Terry gnawed on a thumbnail. "What if it's a virus?" he asked.

"What if it's a program that makes the computer self-destruct?" Stuart said. He made a booming noise and tossed a little mushroom cloud of sunflower seeds toward the monitor.

"Or makes the whole world self-destruct," the Jacobs said together and then fist-bumped.

"Aw, yeah," Stuart said excitedly. "And there will be, like, tidal waves and lava pits and stuff, and the only people who can save the world are the Forest Shade Middle School Rallying Robo-Raccoons." He pretend-punched something only he could see in front of him.

"Stop talking about destruction," Mikayla said. "It's bad for the complexion. Plus, if the computer destructs, our software will be gone, and need I remind you we haven't written a single program yet? We do have a tournament in a few weeks, you know."

"Not if the world is gone," Stuart said. He tossed another mushroom cloud of seeds at Mikayla. She rolled her eyes and turned back to Mr. Terry.

"I agree with Luke. Just open it and see what happens," she said.

Mr. Terry looked uncertain. His finger hovered over the mouse for so long, we all leaned in another six inches. And then, finally, with agonizing slowness, he clicked.

The screen went blank and we all gasped.

But then there was a blip of light. And another. And some static. And then, it flickered on with the worst possible image.

Worse than the computer self-destructing. Worse than the world self-destructing and the tidal waves and the mushroom clouds and even worse than Stuart's wimpy air punch.

It was Missy Farnham's face.

Right in the middle of our computer screen, smiling that smug Missy the Cruel smile, her head tilted in that I-beat-you-again Missy the Cruel tilt. We all gasped again.

And then she started to speak.

"Hello, Forest Shade robo-losers. As you can see, my superior computer skills have allowed me to hack into your program. To be short about it, you have to watch this video if you want to get into your robotics files. Cool, huh? My guess is you probably broke the computer trying to figure out what was wrong with it. Or thought it was going to do something stupid like self-destruct or blow up the world or something."

She shook her head like we were pathetic, an action that somehow managed to be just as infuriating on video as it was in person.

"So the reason I'm recording this video is to tell you a few things. One, you're losers. Except for maybe you, Mikayla."

Mikayla beamed.

"You're actually just annoying and your toe skills are dumb, but you're not a loser."

Mikayla's face fell.

"But the rest of you? Definitely losers. Especially you, Luke Abbott. You're the loserest of all of them. And none of you can deny it, because you go to Forest Shade, and if there's one thing that Forest Shade does, it's lose. I am so happy to be at a school now that doesn't lose at everything. Which brings me to the point of this video. One thing I didn't mention to you guys at the last meeting was that Goat Grove has a new robotics team. Just started this year. Actually, just started right now. By me. That's right, I am going to be a proud Billybot. And I have assembled an elite corps of dedicated future architects, engineers, and computer gurus to complete one mission and one mission only."

She leaned closer to the camera. We all leaned farther away from the computer monitor.

"Our mission: to beat the pants off the Forest Shade Middle School Rallying Robo-Raccoons. And, oh, we will be so successful."

She threw her head back and laughed, just like the evil witches do in Disney movies. I half expected a couple of devoted animal minions to come out of nowhere and join her with toothy giggles, and then for all of them to break into song with purple and black mist swirling in the background.

"Oh, Luke Abbott, I can't wait to see your face when you admit defeat," she said. "Good-bye, Forest Shade losers! And good luck! You are going to need it!"

And, just as suddenly as it had blinked on, the computer screen blinked off. There were a few moments of blue screen, and then our robotics program pulled up.

"Whoa," the Jacobs breathed.

"Wow," Stuart added.

"I know," Mikayla said. "Can you believe she said my toe skills were dumb? How rude."

"Yes, yes, very rude," Mr. Terry said. "But we shouldn't give anything that she said another thought. She was just being . . ." He searched for the right word.

"Missy," I supplied. "She was just being Missy."

Mr. Terry brushed his hands off. "Regardless, we have our program up and running now, so we need to get to work. Who thinks they'd like to give it a try?" He fiddled with his eyebrow, which was starting to fill in with teeny stubs. "Other than Luke, that is."

Everyone stepped back. Except for Lunchbox, who was, as always, slouched in a chair on the other side of the room, totally silent and removed from the rest of us.

"Oh, come on, troops. You can't let Missy get into your heads. Let's rally, just like our name says! It was just . . . what do you young people call it now? Smack talk. It was smack talk. She's trying to scare us."

Everyone took another step backward.

"I don't know, Mr. Terry," Stuart said. "It kind of worked. She's got engineers."

"Not real engineers," Mr. Terry said. "They're kids just like you. Er . . . they're kids, anyway. All we have to do is go over our manual." He looked around, patting the papers on the robot table a few times. "Where's the manual? Anyone seen the manual?"

Everyone took another step.

"It just seems kind of impossible now," Mikayla said. "If

we can't even beat Goat Grove, what's the point? It's so embarrassing to lose all the time."

"I could have sworn I left that manual right here," Mr. Terry said. He lifted a corner of the mat and peered under it, as if maybe he just wasn't seeing a giant book taking up the center of the table.

The Jacobs slumped onto a couple of benches by the jigsaw. "She's right," one Jacob said.

"We're losers," the other Jacob agreed.

"I'd rather be at home working on my toe strengthening exercises than losing to Missy's Billybots," Mikayla said.

"Yeah, I think we should all give up," Stuart said.

The Jacobs nodded.

I couldn't believe what I was hearing. In some ways it was the smallpox invasion I'd been hoping for. Only instead of actual smallpox, it was smallpox of the spirit. The team was falling apart. The manual was missing, not one thing had been programmed, and everyone was giving up, admitting defeat before it even happened. It was beautiful.

So why did it feel so wrong?

If we gave up, if we disbanded and forfeited the tournament, I could go back to playing with Randy every afternoon. I could go to the tournament in November. It would be perfect.

But all I could see in my head was that photo of Dad holding his robot and grinning like he'd just created the best thing ever. All I could hear was his voice: *It was the most powerful time of my entire life, because there were no boundaries. I could make happen whatever I wanted to make happen, just because I believed.*

I felt something begin to stir inside me. A sort of wrenching, adrenaline-pushed roil that began in my fingertips and spread to my chest. It worked its way up my throat, making my ears burn and my cheeks flush, and filled my mouth, and I could hardly believe it, because I was suddenly very aware that . . .

"She was wrong," I said out loud, before I even realized the roiling feeling was spilling right out of me. I looked around. Somehow I'd ended up standing on a chair. I didn't remember climbing up there, but it seemed right. All eyes were on me. I went with it. I swallowed and took a deep breath. "Missy was wrong. Completely. She always was. We are not losers. We are whoever we want to be, because we have brains and we have hearts and we can try. And nobody, not even Missy the Cruel, has the right to make us feel like something we want to do is impossible, because we have every right to believe we can win. There were people in this school before us. They built and they dreamed and they believed. And they lost, too, but think how awesome it would be for us if they had won. Imagine if we went to Goat Grove or James Peterson or Saint Francis and we had a history of winning, so we won all the time because that was what we do. Imagine if we had a whole set of PRETTY GOOD coffee mugs in our trophy case.

"I tell you, people, it is our job to win. It is our job to do that for our younger brothers and sisters and for our children and grandchildren and for any student who will someday attend Forest Shade Middle School. We will win! We will prove Missy wrong and we will be victorious! We will do that because we have to, and because we can! We can all spit in Missy's lemonade together! Now, who's with me?" Somehow both of my fists were in the air, stretching so high above me, my shirt was exposing my belly button. I was breathing hard. I was sweating. I felt great. I let out a victorious roar.

Mikayla and the Jacobs blinked at me. Stuart chomped on a sunflower seed.

Mr. Terry cleared his throat. "Maybe I left the manual in my classroom," he said and scurried out of the room.

"I've got homework," Mikayla said, gathering her things together.

"We do, too," the Jacobs said, following her to the door.

Stuart stood up. "Maybe a little less chocolate at lunch, Luke," he said, then followed the others.

"What? You're quitting? You're letting Missy Farnham win? Just like that?" I asked.

They stood in a little cluster, gazing at one another, gazing at me. Finally, Mikayla nodded. "Yeah," she said.

"After that whole speech, you're just giving up?"

She shrugged. "I guess we are. Oh, well. It was fun while it lasted." She slipped out the door.

"Not really," Stuart said as he followed her out.

The Jacobs just left, shaking their heads in unison.

I realized my arms were still upraised. I let them drop slowly to my sides.

"Really? Quitting? All of them?" I muttered, stepping down from the chair. "I thought it was a pretty good speech." I shook my head and went for my things. "Like Missy Farnham could do any better." I picked up my jacket and shrugged into it. "Her speech was terrible compared to mine. I clearly had the better speech. They'll never hear a speech as good as that one ever again in their whole lives. Quitting. Bah."

I turned and froze. Lunchbox Jones was still sitting in his seat in the back of the room. I'd forgotten about him. He glared at me, his face stony.

I wasn't sure if he'd heard me muttering to myself or not, or if he'd even paid any attention to my speech at all. I wasn't entirely certain that he wasn't about to take advantage of our being alone in the industrial tech room together to get his revenge.

But he didn't move. He didn't make fun of me or say anything nasty. I'm not even sure if I ever saw him blink.

Mustering up all the courage I had, I picked up my backpack, shouldered it, then dipped in a low bow. "Thank you very much," I said and walked out of the room.

# CHAPTER 21

PROGRAM NAME: Shifting
STEP ONE: Robot is lost
STEP TWO: Robot spins in nauseating
    circles
STEP THREE: Robo-hurl

Of all the things in the world that didn't make sense, what I did the next day was the one that didn't make sense the most.

**Things in the World That Didn't Make Sense:**
1. Platypuses
2. My brother, Rob, joining the marines
3. Why "–ough" makes so many different sounds. Rough, bough, thought, though—just pick a sound and go with it, man!
4. Square pizza boxes for round pizzas

5. Why I suddenly and inexplicably, without
   warning, decided to go to the industrial tech room
   to work on the robot after school on a Tuesday
   when I could have been home beating level 42 of
   *Alien Onslaught* with Randy, guilty conscience–free.

But that was exactly what I did. I started to have the idea
that I might do it right after leaving the meeting the evening
before. Everyone might have quit the team and walked out
on me, and Lunchbox might have heard me talking to myself,
but all in all I felt pretty good about my speech. That good
feeling was lingering. And what was more, I kind of believed
it a little bit.

That had never happened to me before. I'd never really
even cared whether or not Forest Shade won at something,
much less contemplated whether it was possible. But now
that I was contemplating, I was a little bit excited. Even
though I think Dad's garage speech had mostly been about me
forgiving Rob, he had been right that believing in yourself
was a really powerful feeling.

And so that evening I began to think about maybe staying after on Tuesday to figure out the robotics program.
Really figure it out, not just slap some program sequences
together that could maim a principal. And by Tuesday morning, I'd made up my mind. I told Dad not to come get me
until four. He felt my forehead and asked if I knew what day
it was, but once I'd convinced him that I wasn't sick and I
hadn't hit my head, he agreed.

In Life Skills class, I asked Mr. Terry if I could mess around with the robot a little after school.

"I thought you quit," he said.

"Not me," I said. "The rest of the team did, but I'm not ready to give up yet."

"Oh," he said. He pushed his glasses up on his nose. "Okay. I've got some grading to do after school today, but I don't see any reason why you can't stay. I haven't packed anything up yet. It's all still in the industrial tech room."

"Great! And Mr. Terry?"

"Huh?"

"Is it possible for just, um . . . one person . . . to go to the tournament?"

He scratched the space where his eyebrow had met its unfortunate robotic fate. "Well, I suppose it is," he said.

"Great!" I said. "See you this afternoon."

After final bell, I sauntered into the industrial tech room, cracking my knuckles in anticipation. I had a lot of work ahead of me, especially if I was doing it all alo—

Hold up.

There was already someone at the computer. And it wasn't Mr. Terry.

The figure was hunched over, clicking the mouse and pressing buttons. But even with his hunched-over back to me, I would recognize that camouflage jacket anywhere.

"Lunchbox?" I asked, still standing in the doorway, knuckles mid crack.

"Go away," he mumbled.

Only it sounded like "Go away," like a normal person would say it, not:

## GO AWAY!!*!!*

(with shattering computer monitors and whirring chainsaws and stuff).

So I didn't go away. In fact, I walked closer. He glanced over his shoulder at me, clearly not pleased that I'd ignored his command, but he didn't get up and roundhouse me out of the room, either, so I figured I was still good.

Instead, he reached over and pulled his lunchbox into his lap, and then went back to work.

I got closer. He was working in the robotics program. He expertly nabbed a box at the bottom of the screen and moved it up top, then tapped his chin a few times before adjusting some of the settings. He reached to his left and plugged a wire into the robot, then downloaded what he'd just done onto the bot. The bot flashed a few times while the data was transferred, and then Lunchbox unplugged it, picked it up, and went to the table.

He placed the robot in the home square, his face intense as he bent over and lined it up just so. I'd noticed the ruler-like marks along the edges of the mat before and had no idea what they were there for, but watching Lunchbox measure his spot with them, I realized they were meant to line up your robot so your program's turns and grabs would work at the right spot every time. He adjusted and readjusted, his movements so slight it was almost as if he wasn't moving at all. He kept looking at a square on the far end of the table. It contained a plastic road sign. If your robot pushed a lever in that square, the sign would rise, and you would get points.

I inched forward, barely daring to breathe. Satisfied, Lunchbox pushed a button on the robot. Its claws opened and closed and then waited.

"Ready position," Lunchbox said, though I wasn't sure if he was saying it to himself or to me. "One, two, three, go." He pushed another button on the top of the robot and it sprang into life, its wires and hooks bouncing as it trundled across the table.

It moved a few inches, turned to correct its course, and then raced full speed ahead toward the square. It was right on target, the claws closing and creating a point that jabbed the lever. The sign went up.

"Yes!" I yelled, pumping my fist. The robot backed up half an inch and the sign fell. "No!"

Lunchbox looked crestfallen, but then he walked over to the bot and picked it up. "I can fix that," he said. Again, it wasn't really clear if he was talking to me or to himself.

"It just needs to push a tiny bit farther," I said, following him to the computer.

"I know what it needs." He clicked some buttons on the program.

"I didn't know you could do this," I said.

He plugged the wire into the robot again and clicked to

download. "Neither did I. I'd never tried before. But after your speech, I figured why not try?"

My mouth flopped open. I followed him as he took the robot back to the table and began the process of lining it up again. "You must be some kind of programming genius or something," I said. "On my first try, the robot went crazy."

He chuckled, his mouth twitching just the tiniest bit toward a smile. "That was pretty funny," he said.

"I could have gotten suspended," I said.

He glanced up at me. The purple smudges under his eyes were starting to yellow a little. "That would have been even funnier."

"Maybe to you," I muttered.

But he'd already lined up the robot and reset it to the ready position. "One, two, three, go," he whispered and pushed the button on the robot's back. It took off again, doing the same exact thing as it did the last time, only at the end leaning half an inch harder on the lever. The road sign popped up and stayed up, even after the bot backed away.

I cheered, but as the robot backed away, it knocked into another square, toppling over a stack of plastic bricks. Lunchbox growled.

He went back to the computer as I restacked the bricks. It was pretty quiet in the industrial tech room, just the two of us, and I figured since he was speaking to me, it would be a good time to get something off my chest.

"Hey, man, I wanted to say I'm sorry. About, you know, the whole door incident."

He didn't respond; just kept clicking.

"They sure don't make bathroom doors as heavy as they used to. I mean, what if there was a tornado, am I right?"

Still nothing.

"But, yeah, I felt real bad about it. About knocking you down and making you drop your . . . your, um, lunchbox. And your nose. And your . . . um, your eyes. Anyway, I'm sorry."

Lunchbox turned in the swivel computer chair and for a second I thought he was going to bawl me out for destroying his face and his lunchbox. But instead he just pointed to the table.

"You gonna bring the robot over here or what?" he asked.

# CHAPTER 22

PROGRAM NAME: The Cog Connection
STEP ONE: Robot runs into bigger,
    meaner-looking robot
STEP TWO: Robot pokes and prods
STEP THREE: Robot is annoying that way

The next day, we met in the industrial tech room again. Neither of us had mentioned it the day before, but somehow I knew Lunchbox would be there without my asking, and I was betting he knew the same about me.

In fact, we hadn't really talked about anything. After I apologized for the door incident, pretty much the only words spoken were "One, two, three, go" and "I can adjust that." I had mostly watched over his shoulder while he worked, occasionally bringing him the robot or resetting something that had gotten pushed out of place on the table. The whir of the robot's wheels was the only sound for most of the day. That and the occasional cheer. Which was always me.

By the end of it, we had perfected only the sign-raising task, but at least that task seemed to work most of the time, so we felt we had done something pretty amazing. Also, most of the jewels that Mikayla had glued on to the robot had gotten knocked off in the process, so all in all we were pretty pleased with our results.

When I came back the next day, we worked on a different task—one where the robot had to spin a wheel to make a yellow ball end up at the bottom. I told him about finding the picture of my dad in Future Club, but Lunchbox didn't do much more than grunt at everything I said. I thought he liked the story, though, when I told him that was what had inspired the speech.

We never got the yellow ball program perfected, but we were close enough that on Thursday, I stayed after school again. Instead of parking myself in the Ultimate Gaming Zone, I was bent over the robotics table, trying to figure out which hash mark to line the robot on in order to get him at the exact spot where his hook would open a latch on a treasure chest in the corner. That task was worth eighty points, so Lunchbox and I were trying really hard to get it.

"So do you think we should meet again tomorrow?" I asked as we both walked toward the front doors at four o'clock. Dad's car was already out front, but Lunchbox was walking home as usual.

"You can do whatever you want to do, but I'm staying after," Lunchbox said. "I'm gonna get that eighty points." Which wasn't exactly an invitation. But he didn't tell me to cram it, stare at me menacingly, or ignore me completely, so I was going to take it as an invitation.

So on Friday we met again, although Dad complained that the maws would likely tear up his entire kitchen when he left at four to get me, but I didn't care. Lunchbox and I were making great progress on the robot, and I was having fun.

Lunchbox was already there by the time I got to the industrial tech room, clicking around on the computer as always.

"I think it's in the rotation," he said as soon as I laid down my backpack.

"Can you fix it? Maybe one degree will do it. And I was thinking maybe we could change the attachment a little bit." It was weird to hear those words coming out of my mouth. They almost made me sound like I knew what I was talking about.

"I can fix it," Lunchbox said. He hooked up the robot and downloaded the data, while I gave the table a once-over, making sure everything was in its place.

He lined up the bot, kicked it into ready mode, then we said the countdown together. He pushed the button and the robot whizzed across the map, heading straight for the treasure chest. It rotated at the last minute, the hook reached out, and the chest flipped open.

This time we both cheered. I even did a little dance, going, "You da man! Who's da man? Lunchbox! You da lunchbox! Woot!"

I got done with my dance to see him looking at me, non-plussed.

"What?" I said. "I'm just cheering you on."

"You're weird," he said, heading back to the computer. "It needs to rotate just a tiny bit less. That was too close."

I tipped the treasure chest lid closed. "What do you mean I'm weird?" I asked.

He clicked the mouse a few times. "Did it ever occur to you that my name isn't actually Lunchbox?" he asked.

"Not really," I said. "Everybody calls you Lunchbox."

"They call me that because of this," he said. He reached over and rattled his lunchbox.

"So?"

He swiveled to face me. "So, do you want to be called Bathroom Door?"

Oh. I'd never really thought about it that way before.

"Well, what's in that thing?" I asked.

"*My business* is what's in there," he snapped, turning back to the computer. "Which you are not a part of and never will be. Just bring the robot over here."

I took the robot to him and he went through the process again. This time the treasure chest opened perfectly. But neither of us cheered.

"We can try the yellow ball thing again," I said somberly. I clicked the treasure chest lid back into place.

He went back to the computer and started working. I piddled around the table feeling guilty, but also thinking if Lunchbox didn't like being called Lunchbox, maybe he shouldn't carry a lunchbox with him everywhere he went. Maybe he should be nicer to people so they don't think he's about to smash their faces every second of the day. Maybe he could do a lot of things.

Suddenly he broke the silence. "Timothy Durgewell," he said.

"Huh?"

"Timothy Durgewell," he repeated. "That's my name. At home I'm Tim."

"Oh," I said. "You mean your last name isn't even Jones?"

He shook his head and laughed. "I have no idea where that came from."

"Oh," I said again, and then, having a sudden need to try out this new name on a guy I'd only ever known as Lunchbox, I said, "Can I ask you a question, Ti-i-im?"

"I guess," he said, and when he turned around it was the strangest thing. He looked a whole lot less mean when he had an actual name.

"Why do you wash up at school every morning? Is it because of the woods?"

"What woods?"

"You know, escaped prisoner, raw squirrels, howling at the moon, that kind of thing."

"No. I live in a house. With three sisters. They're all older than me, and one or more of them is always in the bathroom. It's impossible to use it before school, so I just use the one by the guidance office. Normally I don't have to share that bathroom with anyone. Until you started coming around, that is."

"Oh. That's it?" I asked.

"That's it."

"No murderous rampage or hiding from the police."

"Nope."

"Huh."

He turned back to the computer. "Sorry to disappoint you."

I went back to fiddling with the table. "That's okay," I said, and then added, "Tim." I grinned at him. "Timothy Durgewell. I like it. Tim. Big Tim. Timmy. Tiny Tim. Tim the Titan. Rin Tim Tim."

He gave me a look, one side of his lip curled up. "You know what? Never mind. Just keep calling me Lunchbox."

# CHAPTER 23

PROGRAM NAME: The Almost Brother
STEP ONE: Robot races down mat, excited
STEP TWO: Robot's batteries fall out on
   mat
STEP THREE: Robot conks out midrun

Even though it had been forever since I played with Randy, I was kind of missing Walter and asked Dad if we could have a sleepover Saturday night. Dad agreed, and since I'd been working so hard on robotics, he decided I could spend all of Saturday doing what I wanted, which meant I could do both.

I grabbed a bag of chips and headed to the Ultimate Gaming Zone first thing after breakfast.

Not surprising, Randy was already online. He practically blew out my eardrum when he saw me log on.

"Luke! Where have you been? I thought maybe your system had died."

"Nah, I've just been busy," I said. "What level are we on?"

"Fifty-six. Slow week."

I expected myself to be really bummed that I'd missed so many levels, but surprisingly I wasn't. I was happy that Randy had gotten us so much farther along, especially since he would be competing at the tournament without me.

"I have bad news for you, dude," he said. "Turns out Pluto is a planet after all, and their species is super-tough."

"Really? How did you beat them?"

"Well, their butts are on their heads," he said. "It's really hard to look at. But all you had to do was find a stocking cap and they stank themselves out. It was pretty awesome."

"Sounds awesome," I said, but in my mind I was thinking that stinking aliens out with their own butt smell wasn't quite as awesome as getting the yellow ball challenge with Lunchbox, which we finally did.

"You took damage," Randy said. "Your guy has a weak gag reflex. Sorry. Nothing I could do. It was a nasty battle."

I grimaced. Nasty sounded like the right word for sure. "No problem," I said.

"We'll get you back up to full health before the tournament, though," he said. "Follow my guy into the hive. I think there's a queen in there."

"Hey, about that. The tournament," I said, following his character into a dark room filled with ominous buzzing. "I can't go."

"What?" His character slipped on green honey and fell into a pit. "Why not?"

"It's the same day as our robotics tournament. I have to go to that."

"Oh," he said. "I'm glad I don't do robotics. Seems to really get in the way of gaming."

Normally, I would have said something similar back to him. *I wish I didn't*, or *You are lucky*. But instead I just left it with "Sorry, dude."

"Well, my mom is still going to call your mom. Maybe we can work something out. We'll keep trying."

"Yeah, maybe."

"Now, help me get out of this pit. I think some Plutonians are coming. My guy smells something bad."

We played *Alien Onslaught* for most of the morning, only stopping for bathroom breaks. It wasn't until the doorbell rang that I finally logged off.

Walter stood on the front porch with a sleeping bag, pillow, duffel, and grocery sack.

"Sheesh, Walter, it's only for one night," I said, holding the door open for him to get in.

"Mom sent kettle corn!" he said, holding up the sack. My stomach rumbled. Walter's mom's kettle corn was amazing.

But we were too busy to worry about eating right then. That would come later with scary movies. We dumped his stuff in my bedroom, grabbed a bunch of scrap wood in the garage left over from one of Dad's projects, and trekked off into the woods where the old fort used to be.

I hadn't been back there in ages, but I didn't see any

reason why it would be gone. It may need some sprucing up, but Walter and I could do that, no problem.

It was funny how the woods had changed in the three years since Rob and I had been back there. At the time it seemed like we were in an endless forest, civilization so far away we could disappear forever. The leaves had seemed dense, the trees so tall I couldn't see the tops of them.

But the truth was our old fort was only about fifteen feet inside the woods. It was fall, so there were no leaves, and the trees seemed mostly normal. I could hear cars on the highway in the distance, and if I squinted I could see Dad's clothesline in the backyard. Either the woods had shrunk, or I had grown.

Either way, the fort was mostly still there. It was leaning a little, and some of the nails had rusted and pieces had been blown off. The inside was a disaster, and Walter and I both crept around holding our boards like weapons just in case a rabid animal might pop out at us. But otherwise, it was definitely still workable. Walter and I spent most of the afternoon pounding nails and sweeping and reshaping. He talked about cars, and I listened. Every so often he would say something that made sense, as if I'd somehow been absorbing car facts without even knowing it. First robotics, now cars, what next? Would I suddenly be able to understand why girls hug every time they see each other, even if it's only been an hour since the last time they saw each other?

I was sort of glad the fort wasn't too far back into the woods, because we had to make so many trips to and from the house to find materials. Which, now that I think of it, was probably why Rob had chosen this spot in the first place.

It was on our final trip that we ran into Rob, who had just come home from getting his hair cut. He stepped out of his car, and Walter and I both stared.

"Whoa," Walter said. "You look like an army guy."

Rob rubbed his nearly bald head. "Close. Marines," he said. "And this is just a trial run, so I can get used to it." He looked at me. "What do you think, Luke?"

"I think it's the most horrible thing I've ever seen and they might as well call it the Traitor Cut because that's what you are, and it doesn't matter anymore because Walter and I don't need you, we can take care of the fort just fine without you, so you might as well take your Traitor Cut and go off to boot camp where you belong and where you're wanted," I screamed.

No, not really. Instead, I shrugged my shoulders, looked as disinterested as possible, and said, "Fine."

Rob laughed. "That's it? Fine? I figured you would at least crack one joke about it."

I shrugged my shoulders again, like this was really boring. "You ready, Walter?"

"Sure," Walter said. He put the broom back and grabbed a couple of boards. I filled my pockets with nails.

"What are you guys up to?" Rob asked.

"Nothing," I said, and tried to walk away, but Walter was way too nice for holding grudges against big brothers.

"We're redoing the fort in the woods," he said. "It's really cool. We're going to make a car to go with it. I'm thinking it will be 1963 Corvette Stingray–inspired. I have the Quarter Mile Candy Red paint already picked out. I think my uncle will let me borrow his sprayer. Speaking of, I really like your car. Is it a four-wheel drive?"

"Uh, thanks. Yeah, it's four-wheel drive." Rob's eyes didn't glass over the way mine did whenever Walter started talking cars, but he still looked a little overwhelmed and kept rubbing the top of his head. "I remember that fort, Luke," he said. "It's still there?"

"Yeah," Walter exclaimed. "And it's awesome!"

"You mind if I come back and take a look?" Rob said.

I was almost sure I'd heard him wrong. Rob was asking to come back to the fort? My Rob? The Rob who was happily abandoning me? It hardly made sense.

"I don't know," I said. "Walter and I were getting ready to play Fort Invaders." Truthfully, we hadn't talked about playing anything at all, but it sounded good in the moment to have something going on that left me with no time for Rob for a change.

"We were?" Walter asked, looking excited.

"Yeah," I said. "Remember?" I tried to give him the Say You Remember look, but Walter was way too honest for something like that. He just didn't get deceit. It was probably a really good reason to like Walter, but at the moment it was a little frustrating.

A smile spread across Rob's face. "Aw, man, I used to love Fort Invaders. That was the best game ever. Remember, Luke, how Mom and Dad used to have to go all the way out into the woods and force us to come inside for dinner?"

Yeah. I remembered. It was so great, feeling like it was me and Rob against the world. I thought that feeling would never go away. But it did.

"Hey, I don't really have anything going on right now," Rob said. "You think I could join you guys?"

Walter's face lit up. And I would be lying if I said the thought of Rob joining us didn't make me a light up a little on the inside, too. As mad as I was at him, he was still my brother, and the best friend I ever had. He was still the guy who I made the best memories with. He was still cocreator of the fort, and Fort Invaders, in the first place.

I glanced up at his head, pale where his hair used to be. He was also still going off to boot camp like it was no big deal. None of that other stuff mattered anymore, did it?

I tried to conjure a scowl that best relayed that I couldn't care less what Rob did with his afternoon, as long as he wasn't doing it with me. "I don't think so," I said. "Walter and I have a pretty good thing going on right now."

"It'll be fine," Walter said. "There's lots of room in the fort."

"That's okay," Rob said. "If you don't want me to . . ."

"We do!" Walter said. "Don't we, Luke?" And he gave me these puppy dog eyes that said Walter would never understand what it was like to be mad at anyone in his whole life. It was one of the reasons I liked him so much.

I sighed. "I guess it'll be okay," I said. "But we follow my lead. I get to be the one in the fort and you have to be lookout."

Rob grinned. "I haven't climbed a tree in a long time."

I tried walking back with dignity and nonchalance, but

y

z

· 177 ·

they started racing across the yard, "calling" things, and if I didn't join in, I was going to get the cruddy stuff.

"I get the lava pit!"

"I call the fire blaster!"

"I'm in the big room! I call it!"

We got to the fort, and it was like time had turned back. Suddenly the trees felt tall again, and the highway sounds disappeared. Dad's clothesline looked like serpentine wire around enemy barracks. We were small, because the world in our imaginations was so big.

Rob was clumsy getting up the tree, but his voice cut through the air in barking commands. Walter and I lay on the floor inside the fort and giggled with anticipation, waiting for Rob to yell that the enemy was coming.

We waited.

And waited.

And when the waiting got to be too much, a beeping sound cut through the woods.

At first we thought this was a new addition to the game. Some high-tech alert system that Rob had thought up. We whispered how brilliant it was.

But then we heard Rob talking. And the scuffing and shuffling sounds of him coming down from the tree. We listened, turning our palms up confusedly at each other.

"What's going on? Is this part of the game?" Walter whispered.

"I don't know. I don't think so," I said. "I'll do recon. You protect my back."

"Roger," Walter whispered, alligator-crawling toward me.

I got up on my knees and slowly poked my head through the window. There was Rob, standing at the base of the tree, talking on his phone. I let out my breath and slid back to the floor.

"Phone call," I said. "False alarm."

Rob turned to peer in at us. He covered his phone with one hand and whispered, "Sorry, bro, I've got to take this. It's my recruiter."

Of course. Just in case I forgot for half a second, Rob was there to remind me. He wasn't my brother anymore, he was a marine. A marine who was going to leave, and who had already started leaving long ago. I watched him pick through the woods back toward the house, his "Yes, sir" and "No, sir" echoing toward me. Soon he was gone, and I heard nothing but the movement of Walter's knees and boots on the fort floor.

He pulled himself up to sitting next to me. "Should we wait until he comes back?"

"No," I said. "I'm tired of this game. Let's go inside."

We climbed out and trudged to the house. I hoped I wasn't walking in the same footsteps Rob had just left in the leaves.

# CHAPTER 24

**PROGRAM NAME:** Robo-Rally
**STEP ONE:** Robot gathers other robots
   into one square
**STEP TWO:** Robot traps them there
**STEP THREE:** Robots have no choice but to
   cheer

By the following Tuesday, Lunchbox and I could see a glimmer of hope for the tournament, which was coming up in only two weeks. After some adjustments, the robot was sleek and bling-free, and could successfully perform the sign task, the treasure chest task, and the yellow ball task most of the time. Only every now and then did it repeatedly run into walls or tip over and die.

The problem was, even though we technically didn't need a team, we kind of wanted one. If for no other reason than to prove that we were able to accomplish what we'd been unable to accomplish before.

We stayed after Life Skills class and told Mr. Terry about all we'd gotten done during our practices while he'd been grading papers in his classroom. Well, actually, I told Mr. Terry, because Lunchbox still didn't do much in the way of talking, but he also didn't clench his fists at me or stomp on my head—a good sign he agreed with everything I was saying.

Mr. Terry seemed really surprised. His one and a half eyebrows kept getting higher and higher up on his forehead while I talked, and he kept asking, "Is this some sort of prank? Is Principal McMillan going to pop out of the supply closet any minute now?" The best part: none of his words fell into pits when he asked those things.

"No, we swear, it's for real," I said. "We've got it working. Old Lunchbox here—er, Tim—is a pretty good programmer. Can we still go to the tournament?"

Mr. Terry jumped up out of his seat. "Of course we can. I hadn't ever canceled our registration. We're still signed up."

"We should gather the team," I suggested.

"Yes, yes, we should," he said, clicking a pen and writing notes on a scrap of paper. "I'll take care of that. Wednesday practice is back on!"

The next day, Lunchbox and I were the first in the industrial tech room. We'd discussed it in the bathroom that morning, and we'd decided we wanted to have the robot ready to show off when everyone got there.

We were just placing him on the correct starting marks when the team began to stream in.

Mikayla took two steps into the room, gasped and dropped her backpack on the ground, and rushed to the table. "What happened to Rosie?" she asked, holding both hands over her heart.

"It's not Rosie anymore," I said. "We rearranged things."

"You can't do that," she said. "I put all those jewels on myself."

"But you also quit the team," I said. "And we were the only ones making the decisions, and we decided that the robot was now . . ." I searched my brain, because we actually hadn't discussed robot names at all. I glanced at Lunchbox, who raised his eyebrows at me expectantly. "Tim!" I said. "His name is Tim."

Mikayla looked stricken. "You changed our robot to a boy? I'm not sure if I want to be on this team anymore."

"Maybe this will change your mind," I said. I gestured for Lunchbox to push the button. He reached down and the robot sprang to life, efficiently heading down to the treasure chest and flipping up its lid. It came back to the start square and waited like an obedient dog. I patted what I'd come to think of as its head. Lunchbox had been working on speeding up the robot and making it come home. This was our first run with his changes, and I was glad they worked.

"Whoa!" The Jacobs had come in just in time to catch the tail end of the robot's performance.

"You got it to do something," one of them said.

"Other than attack," the other Jacob added.

I nodded proudly. "We've been working every night."

They oohed appreciatively.

"Make it do something else," Mikayla said. "Make it tip-toe. Make it spin on one toe like a ballerina. Oh, that would be so pretty."

"Well, it's not exactly that easy," I said.

"I thought you said you could make it do stuff," she said.

"Yeah," a Jacob added. "Make it throw a football."

"It can't even pick up a football," I said. "It doesn't have hands. And throw it where?"

"I'm open!" the other Jacob yelled, running through the room with his hands in catch formation.

"I'm not going to . . . stop . . . hold on . . . you guys!" I said as the Jacobs began calling plays to each other, and Mikayla ramped up her whining about making the robot dance.

Stuart sauntered in. "What's going on in here?" he asked, but I couldn't answer because it had gotten so loud. Everyone was talking over one another, Jacob and Jacob running into worktables, Mikayla getting a full-blown wail going. This was a disaster.

And then suddenly a noise boomed through all the other noises.

"Watch!"

Only it sounded like:

(with computer circuits frying and roofs caving in and stuff).

Everyone stopped where they were and turned toward Lunchbox.

"Just. Watch," he said in a much softer voice.

He pushed a few more buttons and the robot eased down the table. It motored over to the yellow ball task, turned, and hooked the wheel to spin it. The ball landed perfectly in place. The robot then backed up, turned, and headed for the square with the sign in it. It barreled forward, pushed the lever with its claws, and backed out. The sign was up. The robot came back to the start square and did what looked like a little dance. I had no idea Lunchbox had programmed it to do that.

"Wow," Stuart said. "That is awesome. Can you show me how to do it?"

Lunchbox nodded and Stuart went with him to the computer. The Jacobs followed, and soon they were all leaning over the desk, pointing and clicking and flipping through the manual that Mr. Terry had brought in.

"What about me?" Mikayla asked, pouty.

"Well, the thing is, we'll have a booth. And it needs to be decorated so it'll stand out to the judges. Maybe some posters with unique art?"

Mikayla grinned as she slipped off her shoes.

And just like that, we became a team.

A real team that planned to win.

# CHAPTER 25

PROGRAM NAME: The Aw Confusion
STEP ONE: Robot prances in front of
 grandrobots
STEP TWO: Grandrobots think the end of
 the world is coming
STEP THREE: Grandrobots crowd robot
 right when he is about to make a move

Because we were only two weeks away from the tournament, I'd started bringing the robot home with me in the evenings to protect it. You know, from robbers, saboteurs, roving pirates, bored ninjas, out-of-control industrial tech projects, Missy the Cruel. I realized I might have been going overboard a little, but Missy the Cruel could be pretty sneaky and underhanded when she wanted to be. So could pirates.

Also, I just liked looking at it. Its final form was a rectangular shape, with shorter pincers tucked inside longer ones like sideways teeth. We'd secured the wires tight against its sides, and put two color sensors on the front that gave the impression of large, glassy eyes. The hook on the back rotated. The whole thing was a solid sleek gray perched on tank-like tires. It reminded me of the kind of robots NASA was always sending up into space.

I'd started to think of the robot as somewhat human, and found myself talking to it as I carried it with me from room to room. I even let it sit in the Ultimate Gaming Zone while I sat cross-legged on the floor next to it.

That was where we were the next time the aws came over.

Randy had some sort of after-school project to take care of, and it was just me and the robot playing *Alien Onslaught.*

"What's this?" Paw Morris said, bursting into the room, his hand already scratching his belly in preparation for his usual position on the couch. "Is it some sort of new sport? What do you make of it, Stanley?"

Paw Stanley squinted at the TV, getting so close he was blocking my view of the game. "Not any that I've seen. Is it some sort of lacrosse? We didn't play lacrosse in my day."

Just then an alien kicked over a fire hydrant into a car and a giant explosion ensued. Paw Stanley jumped backward.

"Holy French onion dip," he cried out, tucking his imaginary whistle into his mouth. "I don't care how tough those Canadians are, that's a foul! Penalty! Five yards!"

I laughed. "It's not lacrosse, Paw. It's *Alien Onslaught.*"

Paw Morris came up on the other side of the TV and leaned in, too. "Alien who-which?"

"Onslaught," I said. "You know, like a whole bunch of aliens attacking?"

"What college do they play that at?" Paw Stanley asked.

"Looks like Syracuse there," Paw Morris said, pointing at an orange alien.

"Seems like lacrosse'd be a more popular choice," Paw Stanley muttered.

Another fire hydrant blew, and the paws jumped back again. "Hoo-eee, that was a good one!" Paw Morris cheered. "Go, Syracuse!"

"It's not a sport, you guys," I said. "Look, it's a video game." I held up my controller and moved the joystick around. I pointed to the TV, where my player ran in circles. "See? I'm controlling him."

They gazed at the controller and then the TV and back again.

"Well, I'll be," Paw Stanley said. "It's a game, Morris."

"Look at that," Paw Morris agreed. "They made a video game out of Syracuse's lacrosse team."

"Oh, brother," I muttered.

Satisfied that they knew they were watching a sport of some sort, the paws took their usual posts on the couch and watched me play, every so often interjecting penalty calls and hoots when they thought someone made a free throw.

"This is pretty exciting," Paw Morris said. "I can see why you like to play it, Luke."

"Yeah, I have a friend Randy that I usually play with," I said. "I beat levels a lot faster when it's both of us."

"Two people can play at once?" Paw Stanley asked.

I nodded. "And we're not even in the same house when it

happens." Why not go ahead and blow their minds entirely, right? "I've never even met Randy in person."

"Oh, that's a shame," Maw Shirley said, having come from nowhere, holding a zucchini in one hand. "Kids these days don't even have real friends anymore."

"He's a real friend," I insisted. "We were going to meet next weekend, but now I can't, because I have a robotics tournament to go to."

"What-ics?" Maw Mazie said, joining Maw Shirley, a drippy ladle in her hand. "Vegetable soup tonight, boys."

"Robotics," Paw Morris said. "You know, they make the robots."

"Oh, my," Maw Shirley said. "Make robots? Isn't that dangerous? You could get diarrhea." I rolled my eyes. To Maw Shirley, there was only one malady in this world: diarrhea. Everything caused it, from overexcitement to influenza. Maw Shirley was constantly on Diarrhea Patrol.

I set down my controller. "It's not dangerous," I said. I considered the Jacobs, who had managed to nail an alarming number of things together since we started practicing again, but decided the maws didn't need to know that part. "It's really fun. See?" I held up the robot.

"You made that?" Paw Stanley asked. He motioned for me to give it to him.

"I helped," I said, placing it on his lap. "And we programmed it to do all kinds of great stuff. And I made a new friend in the process. His name is Lunchbox but his real name is Timothy. You can call him Tim. If you ever meet him. Which you probably won't. But that's okay because he doesn't really talk much. But he's great at programming robots."

"Is he a real boy?" Maw Shirley asked. "Or is he also in the TV?"

"Randy isn't actually inside the TV," I said. "And, yes, Lunchbox is real. He goes to my school."

"Well, I'll be," Paw Morris said. He and Paw Stanley were bent over the robot. I started to feel uneasy, hoping they wouldn't accidentally disconnect something or break off an eye. I made a mental note to add the aws to the list of people I was going to have to protect the robot from. "That's pretty impressive, Luke."

"Thanks," I said.

"And you said there's a tournament?"

"Yeah."

"Can spectators come?"

I imagined the paws sitting at the robotics tournament, their hands scratching their bellies, the two of them shouting about fouls and blowing imaginary whistles, the maws nearby asking the referees who has the better recipe. If Maw Shirley was looking for something that would give a guy diarrhea, the aws at a robotics tournament would definitely do it.

"I'm not sure," I said.

"Well, we'll have your dad find out," Paw Stanley said.

"Great," I said, my voice suddenly finding the pit Mr. Terry's voice had abandoned. I pushed the button to unpause my game and started playing again.

# CHAPTER 26

PROGRAM NAME: The Missing Link
STEP ONE: Robot disappears
STEP ... There are no more steps

It's so weird how things can change really quickly. For example, a year ago, Rob was just a high school kid who didn't even really have any plans after graduation. Today, he was bald and getting ready to start his last semester at home before boot camp.

And a month ago, if you'd told me that Lunchbox Jones would suddenly disappear from school and be gone for a week, I would've been really relieved.

Except Lunchbox did suddenly disappear, and with the robotics tournament happening in just a week, Lunchbox's absence was a big deal.

Monday, it was curious. He hadn't said anything about going on vacation or doing anything weird. He didn't seem sick on Friday. But, hey, everybody has stuff come up.

We went ahead and had practice without him, though we spent most of the time trying to peel chewed gum off one of the robot's sensors and arguing over who put it there (my theory: one of the Jacobs. Although it was entirely possible that the ninjas had found a way in while I slept. Ninjas were good at that kind of thing).

By Tuesday when I found the bathroom empty in the morning, I started to get a little concerned. I kept checking Lunchbox's desk in Life Skills class, as if he might have been there and I might have just not been seeing all 795 pounds of solid muscle that was Lunchbox Jones.

Tuesday afternoon in practice, one of the Jacobs reprogrammed the treasure chest task. Now, instead of opening the chest, the robot scooped it up off the table and flung it across the room.

By Wednesday, I was in full freak-out mode, and spent most of first period sitting on the radiator in the boys' room, staring at the door, using mind powers to bring Lunchbox back to school. Even Mr. Terry had no idea where Lunchbox was. Wednesday in practice, Stuart broke the rotating hook. Mikayla painted the robot's "fingernails" bright pink. And now the robot smashed the treasure chest repeatedly until the lid flung off and landed on the lever that raised the sign. We argued over whether we'd still get the points for the sign.

By Thursday, my stomach hurt from panic. Lunchbox wasn't going to show up, and our team was falling to pieces. Now every program resulted in the robot shivering uncontrollably, making a gargly belching sound, and dropping half its parts on the mat. I may have cried a little on the ride home.

By Friday, I was full-on mad about it. Lunchbox had deserted us, with no explanation whatsoever. Even Missy the Cruel had the courtesy to warn us she was moving. I no longer cared what was going on that had kept Lunchbox away. He knew we couldn't do this without him. You don't just abandon your team like that.

You don't abandon your friends.

Instead of going to practice, I called Dad and had him pick me up.

I was done wondering what was going on.

I was going to Lunchbox's house to find out for myself.

# CHAPTER 27

PROGRAM NAME: The Big Bot
   Smackdown
STEP ONE: Robot gets mad
STEP TWO: Robot confronts other robot
STEP THREE: Both bots explode into one
   billion bot pieces

Even though there was a lot of speculation about Lunchbox living in the woods with the raw squirrels and in caves with angry bears and in prisons and juvenile detention facilities, it didn't take much asking around to find someone who knew where he actually did live.

A girl in my art class knew. Her mom cleaned the house next door to Lunchbox's home. She'd seen Lunchbox outside in the front yard lots of times. Doing normal kid things, not punching holes through tree trunks or anything. (I asked.)

I had Dad drive me there and wait in the car while I went up to the door. I told him to leave the engine running, though, just in case Lunchbox had something really contagious or a pack of feral ferrets answered the door and I needed a quick getaway.

But there were no feral ferrets, and, in fact, the whole house seemed a lot less terrifying than I'd expected it to. It was run down—the paint peeling, dead flowers in window boxes, mud-crusted shoes on the front porch—but there were no massive, pulsating spider nests on the door or bloody ski masks on the patio furniture or ominous music piping in. It looked like a house that might have once been really nice but had been let go.

The door was answered by a girl who looked like a slightly older girl version of Lunchbox. Her hair was brown and kind of frizzy and her cheeks were red and plump. She looked like she could pluck your head right off your shoulders and eat it like an apple if she wanted to. And she looked like she might have wanted to.

"Yuh?" she asked through the screen.

"Is Lunchb— I mean, is Tim home?"

"Yuh," she said. She closed the door. At first I didn't know what to do. Was I supposed to follow her? Was she coming back? Did she think I was just asking to ask?

But soon the door opened again and there was Lunchbox. Or someone who looked like Lunchbox, only a lot paler and sicklier. He was wearing a plain white T-shirt and a pair of flannel pajama pants. Maybe he really was sick after all.

"What are you doing here?" he asked.

"Hey," I said. "I was just wondering if you . . . were okay."

He peered at me through the screen. "Why?"

"You haven't been at school all week."

"Oh." He stood there a moment longer, seeming to feel tortured about something, and then finally opened the door. "You can come in."

I took a step back, squeezing my nose shut with my thumb and finger and covering my mouth with my palm. "No way. Are you contagious?"

He rolled his eyes. "I'm not sick, dummy. Just come in."

I glanced back at Dad. He was already reading a book in the driver's seat. I shrugged and followed Lunchbox into his house.

The inside of the house pretty much matched the outside. It was clean and bright, but looked like it had been a while since it had been updated. The sofa had a ripped cushion. A chair in the kitchen was missing two spindles. The refrigerator rattled. Two more Lunchbox lookalikes were sprawled on the floor, watching TV.

"Get out of the way, Tim," one of the girls snapped. "I can't see."

We walked past them and down a short hallway into a bedroom. It was hot in the bedroom, closed-up feeling, and smelled kind of like rotten feet. Or pork chops. I couldn't quite figure out which. It was a shame when a smell could either be something horrible or food. You were never quite sure if you should enjoy it or not.

Lunchbox shut the door and plopped down on his bed.

He didn't say anything or do anything. He just lay there staring at the ceiling. His nose and eyelids looked red.

"So you're not sick?" I asked, running my fingers along the spines of some books on a shelf, trying to look casual.

He shook his head.

"Have you been out of town?"

Again, he shook his head.

"Funeral?" I tried.

Nope. Nothing.

I turned away from the books and faced him full on. "Why have you been gone, then?"

He shrugged, wordless.

"The tournament is tomorrow, you know," I said.

"So?" He continued to stare at the ceiling.

"So? So the team needs you. We're a disaster. One of the Jacobs got a Tic Tac stuck inside the gyro sensor, and Mikayla sewed a dress for the robot in Family Sciences class."

"Oh."

I reeled. "Oh? Oh! Our robot is wearing a dress! And it literally does not know which way is up anymore. The team is destroying all our hard work, and all you have to say is oh? What are we going to do tomorrow? How will you ever fix everything in time?"

He pulled himself to sitting. "I won't."

I blinked. "What do you mean you won't?"

"I'm not going," he said.

"You have to go. You're the only one who knows how to

program. We need you. Remember me, the guy who shaved off Mr. Terry's eyebrow? You can't leave it up to me, man. I'm a menace."

He picked a piece of lint off his pants. "I'm sorry. I can't."

"Why not?"

"Because I just can't, okay?" He let out an agitated gust of breath. "It was a bad idea for you to come here. I shouldn't have let you in. I'm sick." He let out a weak cough.

"No, you're not," I said. "You already told me you weren't. That cough was fake."

"I have homework," he said.

"You haven't been at school," I reminded him.

"I have to feed the fish," he said, gesturing over his shoulder toward a dried-up aquarium.

I walked over to the fish tank and pulled out a handful of gravel, then let it drop back down into the empty tank with a clatter. "You don't have any fish." I tried not to think about where the fish that had once been in the tank had gone. I wiped my palm down the leg of my jeans just to be safe.

Lunchbox got an annoyed crease in his brow. "I have stuff to do, okay? You should leave." He got up and reached for the door.

But out of nowhere a wave of courage surged through me. I wasn't going to let Lunchbox Jones scare me anymore. He couldn't tell me what to do. I came to his house to get answers, and I wasn't going to leave until I got them. "No way. I'm not going anywhere until you tell me why you quit the team."

He tried to skirt around me, but I moved with him. He went the other way; I went the other way. We looked a little like we were dancing, and it probably looked a little silly, but I didn't care. He took a menacing step forward.

"Get out," he said.

I stood my ground. For the first time ever, his voice didn't scare me. Actually, I was starting to get really mad all over again. I felt like he owed me some sort of explanation, and why would he invite me back to his bedroom if all he was going to do was pretend I didn't exist? Suddenly, it was as if Lunchbox's silence was nothing but selfish. And not just today; every day. Why couldn't he answer questions or participate in discussions or do things that made him seem more normal? Why was he always so creepy, and why did we all let him be that way?

"No," I said.

Only it sounded like:

"No."

(Not everybody can muster a Lunchbox-scary voice, you know.)

"Not until you tell me what's going on," I said.

He let out a deep sigh and went back to his bed. "Why do you have to know? Because of our dumb team? So what if we lose? We're Forest Shade Middle School. Losing is all we ever do."

"It's not about that," I said. "I have to know because you're my friend." It was out of my mouth before I could really consider it. But once it was out, I realized it was true.

Somehow, in all of this, Lunchbox Jones, the scariest kid in school, had become my friend, and finding out why he'd gone missing had become less about robotics and more about making sure he was okay. "I mean . . . well, yeah, because you're my friend," I repeated.

He gave me a funny look—part confused, part mad. "No, I'm not."

"Yes, you are," I said.

"No, I'm not," he said.

"Yes, you are. What about all those times in the industrial tech room when we were alone and you didn't get revenge on me for smashing your face with the bathroom door?"

"I was busy doing other things," he said. His face had grown really red.

"That's not true," I said. "Just admit it."

He rolled his eyes. "Beating you up would be boring."

I pointed at him. "Uh-uh, I don't believe it. You didn't kill me because you like me. Just say it. We're friends."

He glared at me, the whites of his eyes looking a little bloodshot. "No. We're not."

"Say it!" I said again, my voice rising.

He stood up. "No!"

"Fine! Then just tell me why you haven't been at school! That's all I really wanted to know, anyway!" I was shouting now.

He gritted his teeth at me, his cheeks trembling. "I don't want to talk about it!"

"What are you afraid of, huh? What's the big deal? Did you get an F on a test? Did you forget to do your homework for a month?"

Sweat popped out on his forehead. If he were a cartoon, any minute a train whistle would sound and smoke would jet out of his ears.

I charged on, feeling like I was on a roll. "Are you scared? Is that it? Are you afraid to go to school? Come on, how bad can it possibly be? Did you trip on the stairs? Did your pants fall down in the lunchroom? Did you fall asleep and drool on your lunchbox?" He clenched his fists. "Is it a girl?" He was breathing hard through his teeth. At last I had the upper hand on Lunchbox Jones, and I wasn't about to let it go easily. "Oh, it *is* a girl! Is Lunchbox Jones all smoochy smoochy about a girl?" I wrapped my arms around my torso and started wiggling my hips and making kissing noises. *"Mwah! Mwah! Mwah!"*

# I LOST MY LUNCHBOX, OKAY?!

He yelled it so loud, I almost fell over. He was breathing really hard now, and he paced in small circles in front of his bed, kind of reminding me of a bull. "I lost my lunchbox," he repeated.

If my mouth had fallen any farther open, it would have broken my shoe. All this? Because of his silly lunchbox?

My smooch-dance arms dropped to my sides. "That's it?" I asked. "You've missed a whole week of school and abandoned your robotics team on the most important week of the season because you lost your lunchbox? What are you, five?"

He was back to the not-answering thing, which only made me even madder at him.

"Maybe you can bring a security blanket to school instead," I jeered. "Maybe you can tie a pacifier to your collar. Maybe your mommy will come burp you at lunchtime. Maybe you can—"

"It had important things in it, okay?" he shouted, interrupting me. He abruptly stopped pacing and flopped back onto his bed. He covered his sweat-slick forehead with his palm.

I put my hands on my hips. "What kind of important things? What do you keep in that thing, anyway? What could be so important?"

"None of your business," Lunchbox yelled, but the yell kind of tapered off at the end. He took a deep breath, and then, softer. "It had pictures in it."

"What kind of pictures? Like, drawings?"

He rubbed his forehead, clenching his eyes tight. "Photographs, if you must know."

"So?"

"So, they were of my dad, okay?"

I was in mad mode and having a hard time getting out of it. None of this made sense. "Then ask your dad for some new ones."

"I can't," he said angrily.

"Why not?" I said, leaning forward, my hands on my hips. "Where is he? I'll take pictures of him myself, if it means you'll be at the tournament."

He opened his eyes and leveled them at me. Now they were both red and watery. "My dad died," he said.

I slowly sat on the bed next to him. "Oh," I said, the anger zapped right out of me so quickly I felt weak.

"He died when I was seven."

"Seven," I repeated. I tried to imagine a seven-year-old Lunchbox Jones and couldn't do it. "I'm sorry. I didn't know."

"He was, like, my best friend, even though I didn't get to see him a lot. He used to send me pictures whenever he could, and every time we got one, my mom put it in my lunchbox so it would be like having lunch with my dad. And then one day I came home from school and my mom was crying. And she told me that he died. And the only thing I could think of was that I wouldn't get any more pictures from my dad. So I took all the pictures he'd ever sent me and put them in my lunchbox and they've been there ever since." He sniffed, though no tears had fallen. "And now they're gone. All of them. I was so stupid to put them in one place like that."

I perched awkwardly on the edge of Lunchbox's bed, feeling numb and sad and sorry. I'd never met a kid whose dad had died before, and it felt awful. We were both quiet for a long time.

"How did he die?" I finally asked.

At first he didn't answer, and I worried that I'd asked one too many questions, that I'd finally pushed Lunchbox too far. But then he slowly got up and walked over to his dresser. He opened the top drawer and pulled out a wooden box. He lifted the lid and handed the box to me. Inside was lined with blue velvet, and filled with badges and ribbons. I ran my fingers over a gold star attached to a red, white, and blue ribbon. Inside the gold star was a smaller silver star. Lunchbox reached in and flipped the star over. The other side had the words: GALLANTRY IN ACTION. And engraved beneath that, in fancier script: LIONEL C. DURGEWELL.

"Is that your dad?" I asked.

Lunchbox nodded, taking the box and putting it back in his drawer. "Army. That's why I didn't get to see him much. He was deployed in Afghanistan. He was killed there."

I felt like someone was sitting on my chest. It all made sense now—the camouflage jacket, the way the house looked rundown, the silence, the anger. Why didn't I see it all before? Of course there was something in that lunchbox that was precious to him. Why else would he be carrying it all through middle school?

He shut the drawer and made his way back to the bed. All of a sudden the air seemed so heavy and quiet. I felt like a jerk for yelling at him, even if I had no way of knowing the real story behind the lunchbox.

"So I'm sorry I'm letting the team down," he said. "But do you know why I'm even on the team in the first place?"

I shook my head. My best working theory was that it had

been court-ordered community service for one of his many violent crimes, but in light of all that I now knew about Lunchbox and his dad, it didn't seem like a good time to float theories.

"Mrs. Talbott made me," he said.

"The guidance counselor? Why?"

"Because I spend too much time alone and it makes my mom worry, and Mrs. Talbott thinks being on a team will help me get friends."

"Mr. Terry made me join because I'm a video game master," I offered, and then kicked myself for sounding so braggy.

Lunchbox shrugged. "So that's why I don't care about that tournament. I don't care about robotics. I don't care about making friends. I already had a friend. A best friend. And he died."

"Oh," I said. Even though I knew why he was saying it, it still stung a little to hear him say that he didn't care about robotics. It had seemed like he cared all those afternoons when we worked on the bot together. And it stung even more that he'd said he didn't care about making friends there, either. What was I—chopped cogs? I felt a little like chopped cogs. But I had a dad—an alive-and-well dad—so it didn't seem so important to argue with him about friendship anymore. "I'm really sorry you lost your lunchbox," I said.

"It's okay," he said. "It's not your fault I lost it."

"Did you check the lost and found at school?"

He nodded. "I've checked everywhere. I think I might have left it at the mall when my sisters took me there last weekend. But mall security doesn't have it, either. I asked. It's just gone. My dad's gone."

"No, he isn't," I said. "Just the pictures are." But I knew what he was saying.

Because his story was exactly what had me so mad at Rob all these months. Not just that he was going to be joining the marines, leaving, and no longer hanging out in the fort with me, or fending off the maws' corned beef hash with me.

It was that he was going to be leaving.

And, like Lunchbox's dad, he might never come back.

# CHAPTER 28

PROGRAM NAME: Tournament Day
STEP ONE: Robot goes to tournament
STEP TWO: Robot sees Robot the Cruel
STEP THREE: Robot prepares white flag

Robotics tournaments were pretty cool. There were tons of people there, all bustling around in team T-shirts and costumes. One team wore hard hats and yellow construction vests. Another team had wrapped bright pink feather boas around their necks. Teams had shiny crowns and top hats and fake mustaches and pom-poms. There was lots of noise, lots of laughing, lots of shouting . . . and in our booth, lots of arguing.

"No, no, no! The banner is upside down!" Mikayla cried, waving her arms around.

The Jacobs peered at the banner and then at each other.

It looked like it had been painted with someone's feet. Mostly because it was covered with bare footprints. "How can you tell?" they asked.

"The artist knows!" she said. "Just turn it around."

Meanwhile, Stuart and I tried to fix the bot. "I think I've got it!" I said, fishing in the gyro sensor with a pair of Mom's tweezers. "Aha!" I pulled out a sunflower seed. Stuart looked sheepish. "Are you kidding me?" I asked.

"Sorry," he said.

I shook the robot. It rattled. I bent back over it with my tweezers.

We'd gotten our schedule. We would be competing in the very first round. Which meant we were sunk. There was no time to fix anything.

"Hey, Luke, want a peppermint?" Walter offered me a striped candy.

I had recruited Walter for our team, because at least he'd been able to build the bot the first time. But so far all he'd done was wander around admiring the wheels and motors of all the other bots. He even found a dad to talk cars with. The way I saw it, if I couldn't even get Walter interested in our bot, it was as hopeless as it was ever going to get.

"No, thanks," I said.

A guy came through with a megaphone, yelling about the first round starting and teams needing to get to their tables.

"That's us, guys!" Mr. Terry said. "Let's give it our all." Mr. Terry didn't have any idea how bad it really was. He still believed we had a chance.

I stood up with a heavy heart. True to his word, Lunch-box hadn't shown up. Not that I blamed him, now that I knew why he was so upset. But I guess a part of me kind of hoped that he might have changed his mind.

"Let's—" one Jacob said.

"Do this!" the other finished for him. They bumped bellies.

Stuart followed them, and then I fell in line. This was it. Ready or not, we were competing.

We wove our way through the crowd in a single line. Mikayla took the lead, carrying a sign on a stick: FOREST SHADE MIDDLE SCHOOL RALLYING ROBO-RACCOONS.

"Make way for Rosie!" she kept shouting, and I was too busy feeling doomed to bother to correct her.

We found our table, and I busied myself with inspecting the tasks to make sure they were all set up correctly. Walter held the robot at the head of the table. A referee stood to one side.

"Ready, Robo-Raccoons?" he asked.

"Sure," I said. "Why not?"

"Ready, Billybots?" he asked, and my head snapped up.

There, standing at the head of the table next to us, was Missy the Cruel.

"Well, well, well," she said, her braids slithering around her head like snakes. "What luck! We've drawn the losers! This is a sure win." She reached over and high-fived a steely-looking girl next to her without even looking. "I see your robot is just as much of a joke as usual."

"It's not a joke," I said. I glanced at our robot. Mikayla had put a frilly flowered dress on it, a spring poked out the side, and one eyeball was dangling by a cord. It was definitely a joke.

"You know you're not going to win, right? We're going to smash your team to bits and spit out the pieces."

I opened my mouth to say something ugly back to her. But then I remembered the things she'd said the last time she came to one of our meetings. That her dad had moved out, and that he was a loser just like us and she hated him and he might as well be dead. And I remembered how Lunchbox had left the room after she'd said that, because he knew what it was like to really lose your dad. He knew that was a pain that never went away, no matter how many photographs and memories you hung on to.

And it was in that moment that I saw Missy the Cruel for who she really was—a scared, sad girl who needed to act tough to keep her feelings from showing. It was in that moment that I felt sorry for Missy and didn't mind that she was probably going to win, because she had already lost something big, and it was something that I still had.

I walked over to her side of the table. She backed up a bit, as if I were going to do something awful to her. The girl next to her snatched up their robot and held him protectively to one side. I walked right up in between them and extended my hand.

"Good luck, Missy," I said, and maybe she could even see that I meant it, because she gazed at my hand, and then at me for longer than usual, before her eyes went all hard and cocky again.

She shook my hand hard, too hard. "I don't need luck," she said. "Not against you, Loser Luke."

Thankfully, robotics rounds are only two minutes long. In that amount of time, our robot managed to get tangled in a ruffle, spin in circles on its side, right itself only to plow backward through three tasks, break an overhead light, and land in the square with the sign task. It made its gargly belching sound and six parts flew off. The Jacobs let out a moan and Stuart hung his head in defeat. Mikayla pressed her palm to her mouth, stifling a cry.

But just as the last second ticked off the clock, the robot emitted a loud farting sound and a seventh piece zinged out its backside. It ricocheted off the referee's clipboard, skittered across the table, flipped its way up a ramp, and smacked into a lever. The sign went up, giving us ten points.

The team cheered like crazy, high-fiving and hugging like we'd just won an Olympics. In some ways, it kind of felt like we had. Even Mr. Terry had tears standing in the corners of his eyes.

Missy's team had completed five tasks on the board. They had four hundred points. They had stomped us to bits, just like she'd said they would. Yet we were the ones doing the celebrating. She looked confused and a little bit angry.

I walked back over to her team and extended my hand again. "Congratulations," I said. "Good match."

This time she stared at my hand as if it were a rattlesnake.

She grunted, turned on one heel, and stomped away, her team following behind with matching upturned noses.

I went back to my team and we all fell into a group hug. Even Walter, who had no idea what was going on. We proudly walked all the way back to our booth, where we celebrated with peppermints for everyone.

We had lost, but something about sticking with it felt like a victory.

I only wished Lunchbox had been there to see it.

# CHAPTER 29

PROGRAM NAME: Celebration
STEP ONE: Losing robot wins
STEP TWO: All other robots
    congratulate him
STEP THREE: Loudly. Very loudly.

We mostly stayed in our booth for the rest of the day, planning all the changes we would make next year. And, yes, I was surprised, too, that I wanted to do it again next year. I was only sad that next year Lunchbox would be a freshman and would be at a different school. But Walter was going to officially join us next year, and that would be awesome, too.

Occasionally, the guy with the megaphone would come through and announce another round, and we would file into the auditorium to watch. Goat Grove was knocked out in round two. Missy growled and tore their team's banner in half, and then dissolved into tears and had to be taken away.

But we spent most of the time getting to know one another.

We watched Mikayla use chopsticks to pick up rice . . . with her toes. Walter threw up a little in his mouth and had to sit by the trash can for half an hour. I probably should have warned him that Mikayla's foot tricks weren't always for the faint of heart.

The Jacobs told us about the space movie they were filming in their spare time. It was called *Reentry* and, from what I could tell, involved a lot of whisper-screaming in slow motion and flailing of arms and legs to simulate zero gravity.

Stuart gave everyone a handful of sunflower seeds and we took turns trying to spit the shells into a Dixie cup, which we'd placed in the middle of our circle. Even Mr. Terry gave it a try. It was sort of like Pencil Stick, only downward and using your mouth, so it was no surprise that I was the reigning champ with eleven shells.

Finally, the guy with the megaphone came through one last time and shouted that the awards ceremony was about to begin. We got up, but before we started heading toward the auditorium, I made everyone stop and huddle while the rest of the crowd filed out.

"Even though we didn't win anything," I said, "I'm still really glad we came."

"Me, too," Mikayla said. "Thanks for not letting us quit."

"Yeah," the Jacobs added.

"Definitely," said Stuart.

"I love you guys," Walter added. We all stared at him, and then cracked up.

"On three," I said. We all put our hands in the middle and counted to three, then shouted, "Robo-Raccoons!" together.

As if on cue, a noise came from the doorway. In plowed a crowd of people, led by none other than Doris—er, Ricky, our raccoon mascot. It was making crazy googly eyes and marching with pep, a strand of yarn trailing out of the straw purse it had looped over one furry arm.

Behind the raccoon was Principal McMillan, and then Mom and Dad, along with everyone else's moms and dads. Mr. Terry's wife was there, too, and the maws and paws. They were all clapping and cheering, waving signs and doing little dances. We ran to them and dissolved into the crowd with hugs and kisses. Dad ruffled my hair and told me he was proud of me. The maws squeezed my cheeks into pulp. Mom kissed them to take the sting out.

Behind them stood Rob, looking uncertain.

He waved at me sheepishly. "Congratulations, li'l bro."

I went to him, the noise of the rest of the crowd fading out behind us. "Hey," I said. "You came."

"Of course I came. Why wouldn't I come?"

He was right. I had been shutting him out for months, but he'd never shut me out. He'd kept trying to get me to talk to him, to forgive him. He'd given me the ride to Walter's house. He'd tried to play Fort Invaders with us. He was being Same Old Rob, really. And Same Old Rob would have never missed something like a robotics tournament.

"We lost our match," I said. "Missy Farnham beat us."

He made a face. "Missy the Cruel who drinks warm drool?" Of course he knew all about Missy the Cruel's antics. I'd griped about her so many times in the fort, he probably had the glue-eating song memorized. We'd spent a whole afternoon coming up with the "drinks warm drool" thing. I'd forgotten about it. But Rob still remembered, and I couldn't help but smile. "How'd that happen? Wasn't she on your team?"

"She moved to Goat Grove this year," I said.

He smiled wide and knocked into my shoulder with his elbow. "Oh, so Goat Grove is the one who really lost, right? By getting her?"

"I don't know," I said, thinking about the look on Missy's face when our team had cheered for our ten points. "Missy's probably not all so bad on the inside."

Rob stepped back. "Whoa. Who is this guy going soft on Missy the Cruel?"

I grinned. "Way, way, waaay down on the inside," I said.

"So far you need a flashlight to find it?" he asked.

"So far you need a submarine to find it," I said.

"So far they can only find it on the other side of the earth," he said.

"On the other side of the galaxy," I added, giggling. "The butt of the galaxy."

"Yeah, now I recognize you," Rob said, laughing, too. But then our chuckles faded and we found ourselves standing awkwardly next to each other again. "You still mad at me for joining the marines?" he finally asked.

"A little," I said.

"I've still got to go, you know. I already signed up."

"I know."

"Sure would be nice if you forgave me before I went."

"I know," I said again.

"You know I'm still going to be your brother, even if I'm sent somewhere far away, right? I mean, that never changes. The marines can do a lot of things, but they can't make me stop being your brother."

Suddenly the clog was back in my throat, just like it always was when I was around Rob. My eyes filled with tears, which was mortifying. It was not easy being a tough dude around other tough dudes when you were getting all waterworks on them. But I couldn't help it. All I could think about was Lunchbox Jones carrying around pictures of his dad every day.

"What if you never come back?" I asked. I looked up at him, even though it meant a tear slipped out and raced down my cheek. "My friend's dad went to Afghanistan and he never came back."

Rob looked taken aback, as if he'd never guessed that this was what I was so upset about. "I'm coming back, Luke."

"You can't promise that," I said, swiping at a second tear before it could reach my chin.

"No. But who can, you know? I can promise that I'll do everything I can to make sure I do come back. Is that good enough?"

It wasn't, but I nodded, anyway, staring at my shoes,

because at least he was trying, and it did relieve me a little bit to know that he wanted to come back.

"I'm not going away forever, li'l bro," he said. "Just for a while."

"If you don't come back, I will be really mad at you," I said, though I doubted that was true. I'd probably be like Lunchbox—way too sad to be mad.

Rob laughed. "Boy, do I believe it! You are really good at being mad! The past month is all the motivation I need!" He knocked into my shoulder again, and I let out a wet, breathy chuckle, glad to feel the clog slide down my throat a little. "Besides, if I never came back, how would I play Fort Invaders with you?"

I looked up at him again, and he smiled. And since I was already crying, I figured it wouldn't hurt to go ahead and hug my brother.

I wiped my face on his shirt, which he laughed about, and then turned back to the crowd. Off to one side stood a boy that I didn't recognize. He was about my age, skinny with light brown hair. He stood with a woman, who smiled politely. I looked at him closer and saw the telltale mark of a headset line in his mussed hair.

"Randy?" I asked.

He grinned. "Yep."

"What are you doing here?"

He shrugged. "Our moms talked and decided we should meet, no matter what."

"But what about the tournament?" I asked.

"We're on a break. Round two starts in an hour. You can jump in, if you want. I talked to the judges about it. I've been playing in the team tournament. Mom's been taking your spot." He shielded his mouth with his hand. "She stinks. I need you."

I turned and Dad was smiling at me, nodding. "Of course you can," he said.

Walter stepped up to my side. "My uncle Reuben can drive you there. We finished the car last night. I believe I promised you a cheeseburger."

"Awesome, Walter," I said. "But I think I'll buy. I owe you at least that much."

Walter beamed.

"Great!" I said to Randy. "We're on. We just have one more thing to do here, and then we can go."

We'd spent so long celebrating with our families, we missed most of the awards ceremony. We got to our seats just as the emcee held up the last trophy, which was smaller than all the others they'd given out.

"Our last award today," he said, "is not a planned award. But we saw something very inspiring this morning, and something that we think embodies all the things that are important to great success. The team receiving this award has proven that it's not always about winning, or being in first place, but is sometimes just about losing graciously. So this award for Most Gracious Defeat goes to . . . Forest Shade Middle School's Rallying Robo-Raccoons!"

The crowd exploded.

Actually, maybe only we exploded. I couldn't really tell. There was so much jumping and shouting going on, and the hazy run to the front of the auditorium to accept our trophy, the photos, the flash of our moms' and dads' cameras, the blowing of a real whistle that Paw Stanley had wrestled away from a referee, it maybe only seemed like the whole world was happy.

And in the midst of all the celebrating, I saw someone else walk into the back of the auditorium.

He stood in the doorway wearing his camouflage jacket, and holding a brand-new white lunchbox.

I left the stage and walked directly to him.

"Never found it, huh?" I asked.

He shook his head.

I pointed to the lunchbox. "What's in there?"

He held it up shyly. "Nothing but memories," he said.

I nodded. It made perfect sense to me that he would carry around a totally empty lunchbox, even if it made sense to nobody else.

"You can add this," I said. I handed him the trophy, which seemed to be perfectly lunchbox-sized. "You were the first one to not give up, anyway."

He admired the trophy, then turned and handed it to Principal McMillan, who had come up behind us, the whole team in tow.

"It belongs in the trophy case," Lunchbox said.

Principal McMillan turned the trophy in his hands, as if he were holding a king's crown and was afraid he'd drop and break it. "We won something," he said, almost to himself. "We really won something." He gazed at the trophy for a moment longer, and then held it up over his head with one hand triumphantly. He clapped Mr. Terry on the back with his other hand. "A cheer for Bruce Terry, for creating the first team in Forest Shade Middle School history that didn't give up."

We all cheered. Mr. Terry's face flushed with happy embarrassment. He put up one finger.

"And we didn't have any rodents as team captains," he added, and we all cheered again.

I got caught in the moment. I put up my own finger and cried, "And cheers for Tim, for being the first team member who wouldn't give up!"

The cheering abruptly stopped. Everyone looked at me quizzically.

"Who's Tim?" the Jacobs asked.

"Oh. It's . . . um . . ." I gestured toward Lunchbox. "You see . . . Haven't you ever thought he might have a real name?"

Nobody spoke.

"It's okay," Lunchbox said. "I kind of like the name Lunchbox."

And everyone cheered again, because it seemed like the right thing to do.

We started to head toward the doors, when Mikayla suddenly made a noise.

"Oh! I almost forgot!" She reached into her backpack and pulled out some rolls of paper, tied with ribbons. "I made some things for you guys." She handed a roll to Mr. Terry, a roll to one of the Jacobs, a roll to Stuart, and a roll to me. "Open them."

We all untied our ribbons and unrolled our papers. Mr. Terry was first to hold his up.

"It's the bot," he said. Sure enough, in bright greens and blues, was a painting of our robot.

"Ours is of—" one of the Jacobs said.

"Us," the other one finished, holding up their paper, which perfectly depicted a scene of the two of them trying to unnail Jacob's shirt from the workbench.

"Oh, wow," Stuart said. He didn't hold up his paper, but we could all see it was a big, bright yellow flower with a brown center. "A sunflower." He looked up at Mikayla. "It's really good, Mikayla. Thanks!"

Mikayla beamed. "I painted them all with my feet," she said proudly. "I'm getting a lot better, don't you think?" We all nodded. She really was getting a lot better. She was actually getting really, really good. "Look at yours, Luke," she said.

I unrolled mine. And smiled.

"Well?" one of the Jacobs asked.

"What is it?" asked the other.

"I can't see it," Stuart said.

I turned it face-out. "It's me and Lunchbox," I said. We were both at the computer, Lunchbox sitting in the chair and me leaning over him, pointing at the screen, my hand on his shoulder. We looked hard at work. But we also looked happy. Both of us.

"I thought you would like it," she said. "I was going to do one of you separately, but it was hard to get a good scene of you two not together. I didn't have time to paint two of them, so you'll have to share."

"I can't believe you did that," I said, gazing at the picture again. She even got Lunchbox's camo jacket right, and the sharp blue lines of his old lunchbox. "It's . . ."

"It's amazing," I heard behind me. I turned. Lunchbox was looking at it over my shoulder.

I rerolled the picture and held it out to him.

"Here," I said. "I think you should keep it."

At first he looked confused, and maybe a little wary, like I was pulling a fast one on him. But then, slowly, he reached out and took it. He rolled it a little tighter, then opened his new lunchbox, tucked the roll inside, squishing the corners a little bit to make it fit, and snapped the lunchbox closed.

"Thanks," he said.

Only it sounded like:

"Thanks."

(with friendship exploding and stuff.)

# CHAPTER 30

PROGRAM NAME: Returns Happen
STEP ONE: Robot hides in robo-fort
STEP TWO: Robot waits
STEP THREE: Bot army destroys enemy
  invaders

"They're coming! They're coming! Man your stations! This is a red alert! I repeat, this is a red alert!"

Rob's footsteps echoed outside the fort door and soon he dove inside on his knees. He wore his full uniform, which Dad said was probably against all sorts of rules and could get Rob in huge trouble, but Rob didn't seem to care. He thought it added authenticity to Fort Invaders, and Walter and I were inclined to agree.

Rob was only home for a few weeks. He'd made it through boot camp, and came home different. He was thinner, leaner, his hair cut even shorter. He said things like "Yes, sir" when the paws asked him questions, and sometimes he got quiet for no reason. Mom said he was probably thinking about where the marines would send him, and maybe he was a little scared, but when she said that we both got a little scared, too, so we always changed the subject real quick and ate our ice creams.

But most of the time he was just Rob again. We hung out together in his room. We played three players in *Alien Onslaught*. We helped each other avoid another corned beef hash cook-off by making up a story about having to go eat pizza with a school group. We were brothers again.

We had been brothers all along. It had just taken some help for me to remember that.

We each manned our stations—Rob, Walter, and me— waiting quietly, our hearts thumping in our chests.

Soon we heard yelling. It got closer as footsteps rustled the leaves. The invasion was coming.

I poked my head through the window. Walter stuck his head through the other window. Rob spilled out the front door. Just as Lunchbox came barreling into view, the Jacobs rained down from trees on either side of the fort.

"Don't let the invader tag the fort! Don't let him tag the fort!" I cried, and everyone went after him, laughing, yelling, bumping the sturdy fort walls, Stuart tossing sunflower bombs from a nearby bush.

"You guys! Stop! You're going to mess up the paint job!" Mikayla yelled. She sat back on her elbows, her feet busily painting the sides of the fort a bright purple. I hated the color.

But we all had to make allowances for friends. Sometimes I thought about when Lunchbox told me that Mrs. Talbott had made him join robotics so he could make friends. She'd been right—he had made friends. But the weird part was, so had the rest of us.

Rob roared and raced through the woods at top speed. Boot camp had made him fast, and Lunchbox had no chance. Rob tagged him easily.

Everyone gathered back at the fort and regrouped, breathlessly lounging about and thinking of new ways to call "not it." After a few minutes, the Jacobs scrambled back up the trees and Walter and Rob and I took up our spaces inside the fort.

Just as we heard Lunchbox call out, "Ready!" a ringtone split the air. Rob glanced down at his pocket.

"You going to answer that?" I asked.

He reached into his pocket and pulled out his phone, then pushed a button to silence it. "Naw," he said. "I'm busy. You ready, li'l bro?"

I poked my head through the window, smiling wide. "Always have been. Ready? One, two, three, go."

# REAL OR FAKE?

Technology moves faster than someone who just accidentally gave Lunchbox Jones two black eyes. There's no telling where the future of robotics will take us. Five months ago, I never would have guessed that I'd someday know what was inside Lunchbox's lunchbox, and fifty years ago, nobody would have guessed that the following robots would ever exist. Or do they . . . ? Are the following robots real or fake?

## A TRASH-CATCHING ROBOT

Real. It's called the Smart Trashbox and was invented by a Japanese engineer named Minoru Kurata. A sensor, placed on the wall, senses movement when something is tossed in the air, and the bot, which is built into a trash can, zips to the exact spot to catch the falling trash. This could take Stuart's sunflower-shell-spitting skills to a whole new level.

## A ROBOT THAT CAN RIDE A BULL AND HOG-TIE A SNORTING RHINOCEROS

Fake. Though there is such a thing as a Robotics Rodeo, it has nothing to do with riding horses or wrangling bulls.

Instead, it's an event where professionals can show off their newest robotics technology to the military. Snorting rhinos are cool, but a robot that explodes land mines? Even cooler!

### A COACH VERDE BOT

Real. Well, okay, technically it's not actually Coach Verde, but there is a bot that will go on a run with you. From the Exertion Games Lab, the Joggobot is a quadcopter that can float around you on a run, maybe even pushing you to go faster and farther. The best part? It will never call you "men" or ask you to join its football team.

### A ROBOT THAT CAN EXPLODE THINGS WITH ITS EYEBALLS

Fake. But if it did exist, I think we can all agree we would never want Missy the Cruel to have one.

### A ROBOTIC TEDDY BEAR THAT MAKES YOU STOP SNORING

Real. It's called Jukusui-Kun (which means "deep sleep" in Japanese) and was designed to look like a cuddly, floppy bear perfect for sleeping with. But this extraordinary bear is designed to keep its sleepmate from snoring. It does this by using a microphone and a pulse-oxygen meter. If Jukusui-Kun's sleepmate's oxygen drops too low and the snoring gets too loud, the bear lightly touches the snorer's face, causing him to turn to a better, less snore-y position.

## A NOSE-PICKING ROBOT

Fake . . . for now. But PR2, a robotic system that can do every-thing from fold laundry to pick up dog poop, has recently been used to help a quadriplegic man do things like shave and scratch itches. Trust me, from a guy who has been known to "scratch itches" on his nose plenty of times, it's just a mat-ter of time before PR2 has a booger attachment.

## A ROBOTIC FART DETECTOR

Real! Created in Sweden's Örebro University, the Gasbot is armed with sensors and scanners designed to detect meth-ane coming from rotting trash in landfills. Some people think methane is harmful to our environment but could be made useful by gathering it up and turning it into a power source. Methane is also one of the gases contained in farts, so one could make the argument that Gasbot is one big old global fart detector. *Woop! Woop! Fart detected in Jeans Sector Five. Commence de-skidmark-ation program in 5 . . . 4 . . . 3 . . . 2 . . . 1!*

# AUTHOR'S NOTE

My family was first introduced to robotics in 2012, when my older son joined his middle school's FIRST LEGO League Robotics team.

We quickly learned that robotics wasn't just about attaching parts and wires to a motor and watching them toodle around a table. FIRST (For Inspiration and Recognition of Science and Technology) is all about encouraging young people to become leaders in the fields of science, technology, engineering, and math, while also building confidence, self-esteem, and a rock-solid core value of "gracious professionalism."

Basically that means we have a great time exploring science stuff and we're nice about it!

In 2013, our family believed so strongly in the principles behind the FIRST program that we got our younger son involved, joined forces with some friends, and created an at-home robotics team of our own. Our team won the Kansas City regionals, and we got to compete in the 2014 FIRST World Festival in St. Louis, Missouri. There were eighty teams from thirty-six countries there. Our team members made friends from Pakistan and New Delhi, chatted with students from South Korea, and danced alongside a team from

Lebanon. We got to watch teens perform traditional dances from their native countries, try all kinds of candies we'd never seen before, and learn a few new words in different languages. We worked hard and cheered loudly and met new people.

Throughout the season, we also worked. We designed and built a robot. We programmed that bot to do really cool things like pick up stuff and knock other stuff down. We invented a device that could help save lives. We explored a fire station. We made posters and buttons and key chains and helmets. We wrote and acted out scenes and chanted chants.

Who knew science could be so fun?

The Forest Shade Middle School Rallying Robo-Raccoons team is not an actual FIRST LEGO League team. And there is no "gracious defeat" award at FIRST ceremonies. But the Robo-Raccoons is exactly the kind of team that FIRST would welcome with open arms—a team made up of students from all walks of life who are curious and willing to explore something new, who encourage one another and find new strengths within themselves, and who, at the end of the day, aren't afraid to tell another teammate, or even another team, that they did a good job.

You don't have to have science and technology experience to be on a FIRST team. Your coach doesn't have to have experience, either. All you really need is some enthusiasm and a willingness to reach out and learn, just like Luke and Lunchbox did.

To find out more about the FIRST program and possibly find or create a team of your own, visit their website: usfirst.org/roboticsprograms/frc.

# ACKNOWLEDGMENTS

Just like the Forest Shade Middle School Rallying Robo-Raccoons needed Luke, Lunchbox, and the others to make their robot happen, I needed assemblers, programmers, coaches, and support to make this book happen. Here is my official thank-you to my "team."

Thank you to "Coach" Cori Deyoe, and to all the coaching staff at 3 Seas Literary Agency, for doing your usual amazing job of suiting me up and getting me on the competition table, ready to roll out of home base with confidence.

Thank you to all the manuscript assemblers and quality-control bots at Bloomsbury, especially Brett "Ro-Brett" Wright, whose sublime editing skills and funky doodles make revisions fun. Also thank you to Nicole Gastonguay, whose beautiful design work gave our book-bot a perfect cover. And thank you to Beth Eller and the awesome sales team for presenting my bot to the world.

Thank you to FIRST Robotics for providing inspiration on many levels. Thank you to Kathy Laffoon for introducing my family to the world of FLL, and thank you to Team #7223 for taking me on an eight-month journey through intense robotics fun. Weston, Jane, Jacob, Rand, and Christopher, you ARE the mighty, mighty 'Shakers!

And, as always, thank you to Paige, Weston, and Rand for always showing up at competition time and cheering your brains out. You are all my favorite.

And Scott, my main bot, you are the programmer who keeps me rolling over all the obstacles. I love you!